THE
REIGN OF LAW

James Lane Allen

The Reign of Law

James Lane Allen

© 1st World Library – Literary Society, 2005
PO Box 2211
Fairfield, IA 52556
www.1stworldlibrary.org
First Edition

LCCN: 2005906517

Softcover ISBN: 1-4218-1573-7
Hardcover ISBN: 1-4218-1473-0
eBook ISBN: 1-4218-1673-3

Purchase *"The Reign of Law"*
as a traditional bound book at:
www.1stWorldLibrary.org/purchase.asp?ISBN=1-4218-1573-7

1st World Library Literary Society is a nonprofit organization dedicated to promoting literacy by:

- Creating a free internet library accessible from any computer worldwide.
- Hosting writing competitions and offering book publishing scholarships.

The Reign of Law
contributed by Tim, Ed & Rodney
in support of
1st World Library Literary Society

DEDICATION

TO THE MEMORY OF A FATHER AND MOTHER WHOSE SELF-SACRIFICE, HIGH SYMPATHY, AND DEVOTION THE WRITING OF THIS STORY HAS CAUSED TO LIVE AFRESH IN THE EVER-GROWING, NEVER-AGING, GRATITUDE OF THEIR SON

HEMP

The Anglo-Saxon farmers had scarce conquered foothold, stronghold, freehold in the Western wilderness before they became sowers of hemp - with remembrance of Virginia, with remembrance of dear ancestral Britain. Away back in the days when they lived with wife, child, flock in frontier wooden fortresses and hardly ventured forth for water, salt, game, tillage - in the very summer of that wild daylight ride of Tomlinson and Bell, by comparison with which, my children, the midnight ride of Paul Revere, was as tame as the pitching of a rocking-horse in a boy's nursery - on that history-making twelfth of August, of the year 1782, when these two backwoods riflemen, during that same Revolution the Kentuckians then fighting a branch of that same British army, rushed out of Bryan's Station for the rousing of the settlements and the saving of the West - hemp was growing tall and thick near the walls of the fort.

Hemp in Kentucky in 1782 - early landmark in the history of the soil, of the people. Cultivated first for the needs of cabin and clearing solely; for twine and rope, towel and table, sheet and shirt. By and by not for cabin and clearing only; not for tow-homespun, fur-clad Kentucky alone. To the north had begun the building of ships, American ships for American commerce, for American arms, for a nation which

Nature had herself created and had distinguished as a sea-faring race. To the south had begun the raising of cotton. As the great period of shipbuilding went on - greatest during the twenty years or more ending in 1860; as the great period of cotton-raising and cotton-baling went on - never so great before as that in that same year - the two parts of the nation looked equally to the one border plateau lying between them, to several counties of Kentucky, for most of the nation's hemp. It was in those days of the North that the CONSTITUTION was rigged with Russian hemp on one side, with American hemp on the other, for a patriotic test of the superiority of home-grown, home-prepared fibre; and thanks to the latter, before those days ended with the outbreak of the Civil War, the country had become second to Great Britain alone in her ocean craft, and but little behind that mistress of the seas. So that in response to this double demand for hemp on the American ship and hemp on the southern plantation, at the close of that period of national history on land and sea, from those few counties of Kentucky, in the year 1859, were taken well-nigh forty thousand tons of the well-cleaned bast.

What history it wrought in those years, directly for the republic, indirectly for the world! What ineffaceable marks it lft on Kentucky itself, land, land-owners! To make way for it, a forest the like of which no human eye will ever see again was felled; and with the forest went its pastures, its waters. The roads of Kentucky, those long limestone turnpikes connecting the towns and villages with the farms - they were early made necessary by the hauling of the hemp. For the sake of it slaves were perpetually being trained, hired, bartered; lands perpetually rented and sold; fortunes made or lost. The advancing price of farms, the westward movement of poor families and consequent dispersion of the Kentuckians over cheaper territory, whither they carried the same passion for the cultivation of the same plant, - thus making Missouri the second hemp-producing state in the Union, - the regulation of the hours in the Kentucky cabin, in the house, at the rope-walk, in the factory, - what phase of life went unaffected by the pursuit and fascination of it. Thought, care, hope of the farmer oftentimes throughout the entire year! Upon it depending, it may be, the college of his son, the accomplishments of his daughter, the luxuries of his wife, the house he would build, the stock he could own. His own pleasures also: his deer hunting in the South, his fox hunting at home, his fishing on the great lakes, his excursions on the old floating palaces of the Mississippi down to New Orleans - all these depending in large measure upon his hemp, that thickest gold-dust of his golden acres.

With the Civil War began the long decline, lasting still. The record stands that throughout the one hundred and twenty-five odd years elapsing from the entrance of the Anglo-Saxon farmers into the wilderness down to the present time, a few counties of Kentucky have furnished army and navy, the entire country, with all but a small part of the native hemp consumed. Little comparatively is cultivated in Kentucky now. The traveller may still see it here and there, crowning those ever-renewing, self-renewing inexhaustible fields. But the time cannot be far distant when the industry there will have become extinct. Its place in the nation's markets will be still further taken by metals, by other fibres, by finer varieties of the same fibre, by the same variety cultivated in soils less valuable. The history of it in Kentucky will be ended, and, being ended, lost.

Some morning when the roar of March winds is no more heard in the tossing woods, but along still brown boughs a faint, veil-like greenness runs; when every spring, welling out of the soaked earth, trickles through banks of sod unbarred by ice; before a bee is abroad under the calling sky; before the red of apple-buds becomes a sign in the low orchards, or the high song of the thrush is pouring forth far away at wet pale-green sunsets, the sower, the earliest sower of the hemp, goes forth into the fields.

Warm they must be, soft and warm, those fields, its chosen birthplace. Up-turned by the plough, crossed and recrossed by the harrow, clodless, levelled, deep, fine, fertile - some extinct river-bottom, some valley threaded by streams, some table-land of mild rays, moist airs, alluvial or limestone soils - such is the favorite cradle of the hemp in Nature. Back and forth with measured tread, with measured distance, broadcast the sower sows, scattering with plenteous hand those small oval-shaped fruits, gray-green, black-striped, heavily packed with living marrow.

Lightly covered over by drag or harrow, under the rolled earth now they lie, those mighty, those inert seeds. Down into the darkness about them the sun rays penetrate day by day, stroking them with the brushes of light, prodding them with spears of flame. Drops of nightly dews, drops from the coursing clouds, trickle down to them, moistening the dryness, closing up the little hollows of the ground, drawing the particles of maternal earth more closely. Suddenly - as an insect that has been feigning death cautiously unrolls itself and starts into action - in each seed the great miracle of life begins. Each awakens as from a sleep, as from pretended death. It starts, it moves, it bursts its ashen woody shell, it takes two opposite courses, the white, fibril-tapered root hurrying away from the sun; the tiny stem, bearing its lance-like leaves, ascending graceful, brave like a palm.

Some morning, not many days later, the farmer, walking out into his barn lot and casting a look in the direction of his field, sees - or does he not see? - the surface of it less dark. What is that uncertain flush low on the ground, that irresistible rush of multitudinous green? A fortnight, and the field is brown no longer. Overflowing it, burying it out of sight, is the shallow tidal sea of the hemp, ever rippling. Green are the woods now with their varied greenness. Green are the pastures. Green here and there are the fields: with the bluish green of young oats and wheat; with the gray green of young barley and rye: with orderly dots of dull dark green in vast array - the hills of Indian maize. But as the eye sweeps the whole landscape undulating far and near, from the hues of tree, pasture, and corn of every kind, it turns to the color of the hemp. With that in view, all other shades in nature seem dead and count for nothing. Far reflected, conspicuous, brilliant, strange; masses of living emerald, saturated with blazing sunlight.

Darker, always darker turns the hemp as it rushes upward: scarce darker as to the stemless stalks which are hidden now; but darker in the tops. Yet here two shades of greenness: the male plants paler, smaller, maturing earlier, dying first; the females darker, taller, living longer, more luxuriant of foliage and flowering heads.

A hundred days from the sowing, and those flowering heads have come forth with their mass of leaves and bloom and earliest fruits, elastic, swaying six, ten, twelve feet from the ground and ripe for cutting. A hundred days reckoning from the last of March or the last of April, so that it is July, it is August. And now, borne far through the steaming air floats an odor, balsamic, startling: the odor of those plumes and stalks and blossoms from which is exuding freely the narcotic resin of the great nettle. The nostril expands quickly, the lungs swell out deeply to draw it in: fragrance once known in childhood, ever in the memory afterward and able to bring back to the wanderer homesick thoughts of midsummer days in the shadowy, many-toned woods, over into which is blown the smell of the hemp-fields.

Who apparently could number the acres of these in the days gone by? A land of hemp, ready for the cutting! The oats heavy-headed, rustling, have turned to gold and been stacked in the stubble or stored in the lofts of white, bursting barns. The heavy-headed, rustling wheat has turned to gold and been stacked in the stubble or sent through the whirling thresher. The barley and the rye are garnered and gone, the landscape has many bare and open spaces. But separating these everywhere, rise the fields of Indian corn now in blade and tassel; and - more valuable than all else that has been sown and harvested or remains to be - everywhere the impenetrable thickets of the hemp.

Impenetrable! For close together stand the stalks, making common cause for soil and light, each but one of many, the fibre being better when so grown - as is also the fibre of men. Impenetrable and therefore weedless; for no plant life can flourish there, nor animal nor bird. Scarce a beetle runs bewilderingly through those forbidding colossal solitudes. The field-sparrow will flutter away from pollen-bearing to pollen-receiving top, trying to beguile you from its nest hidden near the edge. The crow and the blackbird will seem to love it, having a keen eye for the cutworm, its only enemy. The quail does love it, not for itself, but for its protection, leading her brood into its labyrinths out of the dusty road when danger draws near. Best of all winged creatures it is loved by the iris-eyed, burnish-breasted, murmuring doves, already beginning to gather in the deadened tree-tops with crops eager for the seed. Well remembered also by the long-flight passenger pigeon, coming into the land for the mast. Best of all wild things whose safety lies not in the wing but in the foot, it is loved by the hare for its young, for refuge. Those lithe, velvety, summer-thin bodies! Observe carefully the tops of the still hemp: are they slightly shaken? Among the bases of those stalks a cotton-tail is threading its way inward beyond reach of its pursuer. Are they shaken violently, parted clean and wide to right and left? It is the path of the dog following the hot scent - ever baffled.

A hundred days to lift out of those tiny seed these powerful stalks, hollow, hairy, covered with their tough fibre, - that strength of cables when the big ships are tugged at by the joined fury of wind and ocean. And now some morning at the corner of the field stand the black men with hooks and whetstones. The hook, a keen, straight blade, bent at right angles to the handle two feet from the hand. Let these men be the strongest; no weakling can handle the hemp from seed to seed again. A heart, the doors and walls of which are in perfect order, through which flows freely the full stream of a healthy man's red blood; lungs deep, clear, easily filled, easily emptied; a body that can bend and twist and be straightened again in ceaseless rhythmical movement; limbs tireless; the very spirit of primeval man conquering primeval nature - all these go into the cutting of the hemp. The leader strides to the edge, and throwing forward his left arm, along which the muscles play, he grasps as much as it will embrace, bends the stalks over, and with his right hand draws the blade through them an inch or more from the ground. When he has gathered his armful, he turns and flings it down behind him, so that it lies spread out, covering when fallen the same space it filled while standing. And so he crosses the broad acres, and so each of the big black followers, stepping one by one to a place behind him, until the long, wavering, whitish green swaths of the prostrate hemp lie shimmering across the fields. Strongest now is the smell of it, impregnating the clothing of the men, spreading far throughout the air.

So it lies a week or more drying, dying, till the sap is out of the stalks, till leaves and blossoms and earliest ripened or un-ripened fruits wither and drop off, giving back to the soil the nourishment they have drawn from it; the whole top being thus otherwise wasted - that part of the hemp which every year the dreamy millions of the Orient still consume in quantities beyond human computation, and for the love of which the very history of this plant is lost in the antiquity of India and Persia, its home - land of narcotics and desires and dreams.

Then the rakers with enormous wooden rakes; they draw the stalks into bundles, tying each with the hemp itself. Following the binders, move the wagon-beds or slides, gathering the bundles and carrying them to where, huge, flat, and round, the stacks begin to rise. At last these are well built; the gates of the field are closed or the bars put up; wagons and laborers are gone; the brown fields stand deserted.

One day something is gone from earth and sky: Autumn has come, season of scales and balances, when the Earth, brought to judgment for its fruits, says, "I have done what I could - now let me rest!"

Fall! - and everywhere the sights and sounds of falling. In the woods, through the cool silvery air, the leaves, so indispensable once, so useless now. Bright day after bright day, dripping night after dripping night, the never-ending filtering or gusty fall of leaves. The fall of walnuts, dropping from bare boughs with muffled boom into the deep grass. The fall of the hickory-nut, rattling noisily down through the scaly limbs and scattering its hulls among the stones of the brook below.

The fall of buckeyes, rolling like balls of mahogany into the little dust paths made by sheep in the hot months when they had sought those roofs of leaves. The fall of acorns, leaping out of their matted, green cups as they strike the rooty earth. The fall of red haw, persimmon, and pawpaw, and the odorous wild plum in its valley thickets. The fall of all seeds whatsoever of the forest, now made ripe in their high places and sent back to the ground, there to be folded in against the time when they shall arise again as the living generations; the homing, downward flight of the seeds in the many-colored woods all over the quiet land.

In the fields, too, the sights and sounds of falling, the fall of the standing fatness. The silent fall of the tobacco, to be hung head downward in fragrant sheds and barns. The felling whack of the corn-knife and the rustling of the blades, as the workman gathers within his arm the top-heavy stalks and presses them into the bulging shock. The fall of pumpkins into the slow-drawn wagons, the shaded side of them still white with the morning rime. In the orchards, the fall of apples shaken thunderously down, and the piling of these in sprawling heaps near the cider mills. In the vineyards the fall of sugaring grapes into the baskets and the bearing of them to the winepress in the cool sunshine, where there is the late droning of bees about the sweet pomace.

But of all that the earth has yielded with or without the farmer's help, of all that he can call his own within the limits of his land, nothing pleases him better than those still, brown fields where the shapely stacks stand amid the deadened trees. Two months have passed, the workmen are at it again. The stacks are torn down, the bundles scattered, the hemp spread out as once before. There to lie till it shall be dew-retted or rotted; there to suffer freeze and thaw, chill rains, locking frosts and loosening snows - all the action of the elements - until the gums holding together the filaments of the fibre rot out and dissolve, until the bast be separated from the woody portion of the stalk, and the stalk itself be decayed and easily broken.

Some day you walk across the spread hemp, your foot goes through at each step, you stoop and taking several stalks, snap them readily in your fingers. The ends stick out clean apart; and lo! Hanging between them, there it is at last - a festoon of wet, coarse, dark gray riband, wealth of the hemp, sail of the wild Scythian centuries before Horace ever sang of him, sail of the Roman, dress of the Saxon and Celt, dress of the Kentucky pioneer.

The rakers reappear at intervals of dry weather, and draw the hemp into armfuls and set it up in shocks of convenient size, wide flared at the bottom, well pressed in and bound at the top, so that the slanting sides may catch the drying sun and the sturdy base resist the strong winds. And now the fields are as the dark brown camps of armies - each shock a soldier's tent. Yet not dark always; at times snow-covered; and then the white tents gleam for miles in the winter sunshine - the snow-white tents of the camping hemp.

Throughout the winter and on into early spring, as days may be warm or the hemp dry, the breaking continues. At each nightfall, cleaned and baled, it is hauled on wagon-beds or slides to the barns or the hemphouses, where it is weighed for the work and wages of the day.

Last of all, the brakes having been taken from the field, some night - dear sport for the lads! - takes place the burning of the "hempherds," thus returning their elements to the soil. To kindle a handful of tow and fling it as a firebrand into one of those masses of tinder; to see the flames spread and the sparks rush like swarms of red bees skyward through the smoke into the awful abysses of the night; to run from gray heap to gray heap, igniting the long line of signal fires, until the whole earth seems a conflagration and the heavens are as rosy as at morn; to look far away and descry on the horizon an array of answering lights; not in one direction only, but leagues away, to see the fainter ever fainter glow of burning hempherds - this, too, is one of the experiences, one of the memories.

And now along the turnpikes the great loaded creaking wagons pass slowly to the towns, bearing the hemp to the factories, thence to be scattered over land and sea. Some day, when the winds of March are dying down, the sower enters the field and begins where he began twelve months before.

A round year of the earth's changes enters into the creation of the hemp. The planet has described its vast orbit ere it be grown and finished. All seasons are its servitors; all contradictions and extremes of nature meet in its making. The vernal patience of the warming soil; the long, fierce arrows of the summer heat, the long, silvery arrows of the summer rain; autumn's dead skies and sobbing winds; winter's sternest, all-tightening frosts. Of none but strong virtues is it the sum. Sickness or infirmity it knows not. It will have a mother young and vigorous, or none; an old or weak or exhausted soil cannot produce it. It will endure no roof of shade, basking only in the eye of the fatherly sun, and demanding the whole sky for the walls of its nursery.

Ah! type, too, of our life, which also is earth-sown, earth-rooted; which must struggle upward, be cut down, rotted and broken, ere the separation take place between our dross and our worth - poor perishable shard and immortal fibre. Oh, the mystery, the mystery of that growth from the casting of the soul as a seed into the dark earth, until the time when, led through all natural changes and cleansed of weakness, it is borne from the fields of its nativity for the long service.

James Lane Allen

I

The century just past had not begun the race of its many-footed years when a neighborhood of Kentucky pioneers, settled throughout the green valleys of the silvery Elkhorn, built a church in the wilderness, and constituted themselves a worshipping association. For some time peace of one sort prevailed among them, if no peace of any other sort was procurable around. But by and by there arose sectarian quarrels with other backwoods folk who also wished to worship God in Kentucky, and hot personal disputes among the members - as is the eternal law. So that the church grew as grow infusorians and certain worms, - by fissure, by periodical splittings and breakings to pieces, each spontaneous division becoming a new organism. The first church, however, for all that it split off and cast off, seemed to lose nothing of its vitality or fighting qualities spiritual and physical (the strenuous life in those days!); and there came a time when it took offence at one particular man in its membership on account of the liberality of his religious opinions. This settler, an old Indian fighter whose vast estate lay about halfway between the church and the nearest village, had built himself a good brick house in the Virginian style; and it was his pleasure and his custom to ask travelling preachers to rest under his roof as they rode hither and thither throughout the wilderness - Zion's weather-beaten, solitary scouts.

While giving entertainment to man and beast, if a Sunday came round, he would further invite his guest, no matter what kind of faith the vessel held, if it only held any faith, to ride with him through the woods and preach to his brethren. This was the front of his offending. For since he seemed brother to men of every creed, they charged that he was no longer of THEIR faith (the only true one). They considered his case, and notified him that it was their duty under God to expel him.

After the sermon one Sunday morning of summer the scene took place. They had asked what he had to say, and silence had followed. Not far from the church doors the bright Elkhorn (now nearly dry) swept past in its stately shimmering flood. The rush of the water over the stopped mill-wheel, that earliest woodland music of civilization, sounded loud amid the suspense and the stillness.

He rose slowly from his seat on the bench in front of the pulpit - for he was a deacon - and turned squarely at them; speechless just then, for he was choking with rage.

"My brethren," he said at length slowly, for he would not speak until he had himself under control, "I think we all remember what it is to be persecuted for religion's sake. Long before we came together in Spottsylvania County, Virginia, and organized ourselves into a church and travelled as a church over the mountains into this wilderness, worshipping by the way, we knew what it was to be persecuted. Some of us were sent to jail for preaching the Gospel and kept there; we preached to the people through the bars of our dungeons. Mobs were collected outside to drown our voices; we preached the louder and some jeered, but some felt sorry and began to serve God. They burned matches and pods of red pepper to choke us; they hired strolls to beat drums that we might not be heard for the din. Some of us knew what it was to have live snakes thrown into our assemblages while at worship; or nests of live hornets. Or to have a crowd rush into the church with farming tools and whips and clubs. Or to see a gun levelled at one of us in the pulpit, and to be dispersed with firearms. Harder than any of these things to stand, we have known what it is to be slandered. But no single man of us, thank God, ever stopped for these things or for anything.

Thirty years and more this lasted, until we and all such as we found a friend in Patrick Henry. Now, we hear that by statute all religious believers in Virginia have been made equal as respects the rights and favors of the law.

"But you know it was partly to escape intolerable tyranny that we left our mother country and travelled a path paved with suffering and lined with death into this wilderness. For in this virgin land we thought we should be free to worship God according to our consciences."

"Since we arrived you know what our life has been, - how we have fought and toiled and suffered all things together. You recall how lately it was that when we met in the woods for worship, - having no church and no seats, - we men listened and sang and prayed with our rifles on our shoulders."

He paused, for the memories hurt him cruelly.

"And now you notify me that you intend to expel me from this church as a man no longer fit to worship my Maker in your company. Do you bring any charge against my life, my conduct? None. Nothing but that, as a believer in the living God - whom honestly I try to serve according to my erring light - I can no longer have a seat among you - not believing as you believe. But this is the same tyranny that you found unendurable in Spottsylvania. You have begun it in Kentucky. You have been at it already how long? Well, my brethren, I'll soon end your tyranny over me. You need not TURN me out. And I need not change my religious opinions. I will GO out. But - "

He wheeled round to the rough pulpit on which lay the copy of the Bible that they had brought with them from Virginia, their Ark of the Covenant on the way, seized it, and faced them again. He strode toward the congregation as far as the benches would allow - not seeing clearly, for he was sightless with his tears.

"But," he roared, and as he spoke he struck the Bible repeatedly with his clenched fist, "by the Almighty, I will build a church of my own to Him! To Him! do you hear? not to your opinions of Him nor mine nor any man's! I will cut off a parcel of my farm and make a perpetual deed of it in the courts, to be held in trust forever. And while the earth stands, it shall stand, free to all Christian believers. I will build a school-house and a meeting-house, where any child may be free to learn and any man or woman free to worship."

He put the Bible back with shaking arms and turned on them again.

"As for you, my brethren," he said, his face purple and

distorted with passion, "you may be saved in your crooked, narrow way, if the mercy of God is able to do it. But you are close to the jaws of Hell this day!"

He went over into a corner for his hat, took his wife by the hand and held it tightly, gathered the flock of his children before him, and drove them out of the church. He mounted his horse, lifted his wife to her seat behind him, saw his children loaded on two other horses, and, leading the way across the creek, disappeared in the wilderness.

II

Some sixty-five years later, one hot day of midsummer in 1865 - one Saturday afternoon - a lad was cutting weeds in a woodland pasture; a big, raw-boned, demure boy of near eighteen.

He had on heavy shoes, the toes green with grass stain; the leather so seasoned by morning dews as to be like wood for hardness. These were to keep his feet protected from briers or from the bees scattered upon the wild white clover or from the terrible hidden thorns of the honey-locust. No socks. A pair of scant home-spun trousers, long outgrown. A coarse clean shirt. His big shock-head thatched with yellow straw, a dilapidated sun-and-rain shed.

The lanky young giant cut and cut and cut: great purple-bodied poke, strung with crimson-juiced seed; great burdock, its green burrs a plague; great milk-weed, its creamy sap gushing at every gash; great thistles, thousand-nettled; great ironweed, plumed with royal purple; now and then a straggling bramble prone with velvety berries - the outpost of a patch behind him; now and then - more carefully, lest he notch his blade - low sprouts of wild cane, survivals of the impenetrable brakes of pioneer days. All these and more, the rank, mighty measure of the soil's fertility - low down.

Measure of its fertility aloft, the tops of the trees, from which the call of the red-headed woodpecker sounded as faint as the memory of a sound and the bark of the squirrels was elfin-thin. A hot crowded land, crammed with undergrowth and overgrowth wherever a woodland stood; and around every woodland dense cornfields; or, denser still, the leagues of swaying hemp. The smell of this now lay heavy on the air, seeming to be dragged hither and thither like a slow scum on the breeze, like a moss on a sluggish pond. A deep robust land; and among its growths he - this lad, in his way a self-unconscious human weed, the seed of his kind borne in from far some generations back, but springing out of the soil naturally now, sap of its sap, strength of its strength.

He paused by and by and passed his forefinger across his forehead, brushing the sweat away from above his quiet eyes. He moistened the tip of his thumb and slid it along the blade of his hemp hook - he was using that for lack of a scythe. Turning, he walked back to the edge of the brier thicket, sat down in the shade of a black walnut, threw off his tattered head-gear, and, reaching for his bucket of water covered with poke leaves, lifted it to his lips and drank deeply, gratefully. Then he drew a whetstone from his pocket, spat on it, and fell to sharpening his blade.

The heat of his work, the stifling air, the many-toned woods, the sense of the vast summering land - these things were not in his thoughts. Some days before, despatched from homestead to homestead, rumors had reached him away off here at work on his father's farm, of a great university to be opened the following autumn at Lexington. The like of it with its many colleges Kentucky, the South, the Mississippi valley had never seen. It had been the talk among the farming people in their harvest fields, at the cross-roads, on their porches - the one deep sensation among them since the war.

For solemn, heart-stirring as such tidings would have been at any other time, more so at this. Here, on the tableland of this unique border state, Kentucky - between the halves of the nation lately at strife - scene of their advancing and retreating armies - pit of a frenzied commonwealth - here was to arise this calm university, pledge of the new times, plea for the peace and amity of learning, fresh chance for study of the revelation of the Lord of Hosts and God of battles. The animosities were over, the humanities re-begun.

Can you remember your youth well enough to be able to recall the time when the great things happened for which you seemed to be waiting? The boy who is to be a soldier - one day he hears a distant bugle: at once HE knows. A second glimpses a bellying sail: straightway the ocean path beckons to him. A third discovers a college, and toward its kindly lamps of learning turns young eyes that have been kindled and will stay kindled to the end.

For some years this particular lad, this obscure item in Nature's plan which always passes understanding, had been growing more unhappy in his place in creation. By temperament he was of a type the most joyous and self-reliant - those sure signs of health; and discontent now was due to the fact that he had outgrown his place. Parentage - a farm and its tasks - a country neighborhood and its narrowness - what more are these sometimes than a starting-point for a young life; as a flowerpot might serve to sprout an oak, and as the oak would inevitably reach the hour when it would either die or burst out, root and branch, into the whole heavens and the earth; as the shell and yolk of an egg are the starting-point for the wing and eye of the eagle. One thing only he had not outgrown, in one thing only he was not unhappy: his religious nature. This had always been in him as breath was in him, as blood was in him: it was his life. Dissatisfied now with his position in the world, it was this alone that kept him contented in himself. Often the religious are the weary; and perhaps nowhere else does a perpetual vision of Heaven so disclose itself to the weary as above lonely toiling fields. The lad had long been lifting his inner eye to this vision.

When, therefore, the tidings of the university with its Bible College reached him, whose outward mould was hardship, whose inner bliss was piety, at once they fitted his ear as the right sound, as the gladness of long awaited intelligence. It was bugle to the soldier, sail to the sailor, lamp of learning to the innate student At once he knew that he was going to the university - sometime, somehow - and from that moment felt no more discontent, void, restlessness, nor longing.

It was of this university, then, that he was happily day-dreaming as he whetted his hemp hook in the depths of the woods that Saturday afternoon. Sitting low amid heat and weeds and thorns, he was already as one who had climbed above the earth's eternal snow-line and sees only white peaks and pinnacles - the last sublimities.

He felt impatient for to-morrow. One of the professors of the university, of the faculty of the Bible College, had been travelling over the state during the summer, pleading its cause before the people. He had come into that neighborhood to preach and to plead. The lad would be there to hear.

The church in which the professor was to plead for learning and religion was the one first set up in the Kentucky wilderness as a house of religious liberty; and the lad was a great-grandchild of the founder of that church, here emerging mysteriously from the deeps of life four generations down the line.

III

The church which David's grim old Indian-fighting great-grandfather had dedicated to freedom of belief in the wilderness, cutting off a parcel of his lands as he had hotly sworn and building on it a schoolhouse also, stood some miles distant across the country. The vast estate of the pioneer had been cut to pieces for his many sons. With the next generation the law of partible inheritance had further subdivided each of these; so that in David's time a single small farm was all that had fallen to his father; and his father had never increased it. The church was situated on what had been the opposite boundary of the original grant. But he with most of the other boys in the neighborhood had received his simple education in that school; and he had always gone to worship under that broad-minded roof, whatsoever the doctrines and dogmas haply preached.

These doctrines and dogmas of a truth were varied and conflicting enough; for the different flocks and herds of Protestant believers with their parti-colored guides had for over fifty years found the place a very convenient strip of spiritual pasture: one congregation now grazing there jealously and exclusively; afterwards another.

On this quiet bright Sunday morning in the summer of

1865, the building (a better than the original one, which had long before been destroyed by accidental burning) was overcrowded with farming folk, husbands and wives, of all denominations in the neighborhood, eager to hear the new plea, the new pleader. David's father and mother, intense sectarians and dully pious souls, sat among them. He himself, on a rearmost bench, was wedged fast between two other lads of about his own age - they dumb with dread lest they should be sent away to this university. The minister soon turned the course of his sermon to the one topic that was uppermost and bottommost in the minds of all.

He bade them understand now, if they had never realized it before, that from the entrance of educated men and women into the western wilderness, those real founders and builders of the great commonwealth, the dream of the Kentuckians had been the establishment of a broad, free institution of learning for their sons. He gave the history of the efforts and the failures to found such an institution, from the year 1780 to the beginning of the Civil War; next he showed how, during those few awful years, the slow precious accumulations of that preceding time had been scattered; books lost, apparatus ruined, the furniture of lecture rooms destroyed, one college building burned, another seized and held as a hospital by the federal government; and he concluded with painting for them a vision of the real university which was now to arise at last, oldest, best passion of the people, measure of the height and breadth of the better times: knowing no North, no South, no latitude, creed, bias, or political end. In speaking of its magnificent new endowments, he dwelt upon the share contributed by the liberal-minded farmers of the state, to some of whom he was speaking: showing how, forgetful of the disappointments and failures of their fathers, they had poured out money by the thousands and tens of thousands, as soon as the idea was presented to them again - the rearing of a great institution by the people and for the people in their own land for the training of their sons, that they might not be sent away to New England or to Europe.

His closing words were solemn indeed; they related to the college of the Bible, where his own labors were to be performed. For this, he declared, he pleaded not in the name of the new State, the new nation, but in the name of the Father. The work of this college was to be the preparation of young men for the Christian ministry, that they might go into all the world and preach the Gospel. One truth he bade them bear in mind: that this training was to be given without sectarian theology; that his brethren themselves represented a revolution among believers, having cast aside the dogmas of modern teachers, and taken, as the one infallible guide of their faith and practice, the Bible simply; so making it their sole work to bring all modern believers together into one church, and that one church the church of the apostles.

For this university, for this college of the Bible especially, he asked, then, the gift and consecration of their sons.

Toward dusk that day David's father and mother were sitting side by side on the steps of their front porch. Some neighbors who had spent the afternoon with them were just gone. The two were talking over in low, confidential tones certain subjects discussed less frankly with their guests. These related to the sermon of the morning, to the university, to what boys in the neighborhood would probably be entered as students. Their neighbors had asked whether David would go. The father and mother had exchanged quick glances and made no reply. Something in the father's mind now lay like worm-wood on the lips.

He sat leaning his head on his hand, his eyes on the ground, brooding, embittered.

"If I had only had a son to have been proud of!" he muttered. "It's of no use; he wouldn't go. It isn't in him to take an education."

"No," said the mother, comforting him resignedly, after a pause in which she seemed to be surveying the boy's whole life; "it's of no use; there never was much in David."

"Then he shall work!" cried the father, striking his knee with clenched fist. "I'll see that he is kept at work."

Just then the lad came round from behind the house, walking rapidly. Since dinner he had been off somewhere, alone, having it out with himself, perhaps shrinking, most of all, from this first exposure to his parents. Such an ordeal is it for us to reveal what we really are to those who have known us longest and have never discovered us.

He walked quickly around and stood before them, pallid and shaking from head to foot.

"Father!" -

There was filial dutifulness in the voice, but what they

had never heard from those lips - authority.

"I am going to the university, to the Bible College. It will be hard for you to spare me, I know, and I don't expect to go at once. But I shall begin my preparations, and as soon as it is possible I am going. I have felt that you and mother ought to know my decision at once."

As he stood before them in the dusk and saw on their countenances an incredible change of expression, he naturally mistook it, and spoke again with more authority.

"Don't say anything to me now, father! And don't oppose me when the time comes; it would be useless. Try to learn while I am getting ready to give your consent and to obtain mother's. That is all I have to say."

He turned quickly away and passed out of the yard gate toward the barn, for the evening feeding.

The father and mother followed his figure with their eyes, forgetting each other, as long as it remained in sight. If the flesh of their son had parted and dissolved away into nothingness, disclosing a hidden light within him like the evening star, shining close to their faces, they could scarce have been struck more speechless. But after a few moments they had adjusted themselves to this lofty annunciation. The mother, unmindful of what she had just said, began to recall little incidents of the lad's life to show that this was what he was always meant to be. She loosened from her throat the breast-pin containing the hair of the three heads braided together, and drew her husband's attention to it with a smile. He, too, disregarding his disparagement of the few minutes previous, now began to admit with warmth how good a mind David had always had. He prophesied that at college he would outstrip the other boys from that neighborhood. This, in its way, was also fresh happiness to him; for, smarting under his poverty among rich neighbors, and fallen from the social rank to which he was actually entitled, he now welcomed the secondary joy which originates in the revenge men take upon each other through the superiority of their children.

One thing both agreed in: that this explained their son. He had certainly always needed an explanation. But no wonder; he was to be a minister. And who had a right to understand a minister? He was entitled to be peculiar.

When David came in to supper that night and took his seat, shame-faced, frowning and blinking at the candle-light, his father began to talk to him as he had never believed possible; and his mother, placing his coffee before him, let her hand rest on his shoulder.

He, long ahungered for their affection and finding it now when least expected, filled to the brim, choked at every morsel, got away as soon as he could into the sacred joy of the night Ah, those thrilling hours when the young disciple, having for the first time confessed openly his love of the Divine, feels that the Divine returns his love and accepts his service!

IV

Autumn came, the university opened wide its harmonious doors, welcoming Youth and Peace.

All that day a lad, alone at his field work away off on the edge of the bluegrass lands, toiled as one listening to a sublime sound in the distance - the tramping, tramping, tramping of the students as they assembled from the farms of the state and from other states. Some boys out of his own neighborhood had started that morning, old schoolfellows. He had gone to say good-by; had sat on the bed and watched them pack their fine new trunks - cramming these with fond maternal gifts and the thoughtless affluence of necessary and unnecessary things; had heard all the wonderful talk about classes and professors and societies; had wrung their hands at last with eyes turned away, that none might see the look in them - the immortal hunger.

How empty now the whole land without those two or three boys! Not far away across the fields, soft-white in the clear sunshine, stood the home of one of them - the green shutters of a single upper room tightly closed. His heart-strings were twisted tight and wrung sore this day; and more than once he stopped short in his work (the cutting of briers along a fence), arrested by the temptation to throw down his hook and go. The sacred arguments were on his side. Without choice or search of his they clamored and battered at his inner ear - those commands of the Gospels, the long reverberations of that absolute Voice, bidding irresolute workaday disciples leave the plough in the furrow, leave whatsoever task was impending or duty uppermost to the living or the dead, and follow, - "Follow Me!"

Arguments, verily, had he in plenty; but raiment - no; nor scrip. And knew he ever so little of the world, sure he felt of this: that for young Elijahs at the university there were no ravens; nor wild honey for St. John; nor Galilean basketfuls left over by hungry fisherfolk, fishers of men.

So back to his briers. And back to the autumn soil, days of hard drudging, days of hard thinking. The chief problem for the nigh future being, how soonest to provide the raiment, fill the scrip; and so with time enough to find out what, on its first appearance, is so terrible a discovery to the young, straining against restraint: that just the lack of a coarse garment or two - of a little money for a little plain food - of a few candles and a few coverlets for light and warmth with a book or two thrown in - that a need so poor, paltry as this, may keep mind and heart back for years. Ah, happy ye! with whom this last not too long - or for always!

Yet happy ye, whether the waiting be for short time or long time, if only it bring on meanwhile, as it brought on with him, the struggle! One sure reward ye have, then, as he had, though there may be none other - just the struggle: the marshalling to the front of rightful forces - will, effort, endurance, devotion; the putting resolutely back of forces wrongful; the hardening of all

James Lane Allen

that is soft within, the softening of all that is hard: until out of the hardening and the softening results the better tempering of the soul's metal, and higher development of those two qualities which are best in man and best in his ideal of his Maker - strength and kindness, power and mercy. With an added reward also, if the struggle lead you to perceive (what he did not perceive), as the light of your darkness, the sweet of bitter, that real struggling is itself real living, and that no ennobling thing of this earth is ever to be had by man on any other terms: so teaching him, none too soon, that any divine end is to be reached but through divine means, that a great work requires a great preparation.

Of the lad's desperate experience henceforth in mere outward matters the recital may be suppressed: the struggle of the earth's poor has grown too common to make fresh reading. He toiled direfully, economized direfully, to get to his college, but in this showed only the heroism too ordinary among American boys to be marvelled at more. One fact may be set down, as limning some true figure of him on the landscape of those years in that peculiar country.

The war had just closed. The farmers, recollecting the fortunes made in hemp before, had hurried to the fields. All the more as the long interruption of agriculture in the South had resulted in scarcity of cotton; so that the earnest cry came to Kentucky for hemp at once to take many of its places. But meantime the slaves had been set free: where before ordered, they must now be hired. A difficult agreement to effect at all times, because will and word and bond were of no account. Most difficult when the breaking of hemp was to be bargained for; since the laborer is kept all day in the winter fields, away from the fireside, and must toil solitary at his brake, cut off from the talk and laughter which lighten work among that race. So that wages rose steadily, and the cost of hemp with them.

The lad saw in this demand for the lowest work at the highest prices his golden opportunity - and seized it. When the hemp-breaking season opened that winter, he made his appearance on the farm of a rich farmer near by, taking his place with the negroes.

There is little art in breaking hemp. He soon had the knack of that: his muscles were toughened already. He learned what it was sometimes to eat his dinner in the fields, warming it, maybe, on the coals of a stump set on fire near his brake; to bale his hemp at nightfall and follow the slide or wagon to the barn; there to wait with the negroes till it was weighed on the steelyards; and at last, with muscles stiff and sore, throat husky with dust, to stride away rapidly over the bitter darkening land to other work awaiting him at home.

Had there been call to do this before the war, it might not have been done. But now men young and old, who had never known what work was, were replacing their former slaves. The preexisting order had indeed rolled away like a scroll; and there was the strange fresh universal stir of humanity over the land like the stir of nature in a boundless wood under a new spring firmament He was one of a multitude of new toilers; but the first in his neighborhood, and alone in his grim choice of work.

So dragged that winter through. When spring returned, he did better. With his father's approval, he put in some acres for himself - sowed it, watched it, prayed for it; in summer cut it; with hired help stacked it in autumn;

broke it himself the winter following; sold it the next spring; and so found in his pocket the sorely coveted money.

This was increased that summer from the sale of cord wood, through driblets saved by his father and mother; and when, autumn once more advanced with her days of shadow and thoughtfulness - two years having now passed - he was in possession of his meagre fortune, wrung out of earth, out of sweat and strength and devotion.

Only a few days remained now before his leaving for the university - very solemn tender days about the house with his father and mother.

And now for the lad's own sake, as for the clearer guidance of those who may care to understand what so incredibly befell him afterward, an attempt must be made to reveal somewhat of his spiritual life during those two years. It was this, not hard work, that writ his history.

As soon as he had made up his mind to study for the ministry, he had begun to read his Bible absorbingly, sweeping through that primitive dawn of life among the Hebrews and that second, brilliant one of the Christian era. He had few other books, none important; he knew nothing of modern theology or modern science. Thus he was brought wholly under the influence of that view of Man's place in Nature which was held by the earliest Biblical writers, has imposed itself upon countless millions of minds since then, and will continue to impose itself - how much longer?

As regarded, then, his place in Nature, this boy became

a contemporary of the Psalmist; looked out upon the physical universe with the eye of Job; placed himself back beside that simple, audacious, sublime child - Man but awakening from his cradle of faith in the morning of civilization. The meaning of all which to him was this: that the most important among the worlds swung in space was the Earth, on account of a single inhabitant - Man. Its shape had been moulded, its surface fitted up, as the dwelling-place of Man. Land, ocean, mountain-range, desert, valley - these were designed alike for Man. The sun - it was for him; and the moon; and the stars, hung about the earth as its lights - guides to the mariner, reminders to the landsman of the Eye that never slumbered. The clouds - shade and shower - they were mercifully for Man. Nothing had meaning, possessed value, save as it derived meaning and value from him. The great laws of Nature - they, too, were ordered for Man's service, like the ox and the ass; and as he drove his ox and his ass whither he would, caused them to move forward or to stop at the word of command, so Man had only to speak properly (in prayer) and these laws would move faster or less fast, stop still, turn to the right or the left side of the road that he desired to travel. Always Man, Man, Man, nothing but Man! To himself measure of the universe as to himself a little boy is sole reason for the food and furnishings of his nursery.

This conception of Man's place in Nature has perhaps furnished a very large part of the history of the world. Even at this close of the nineteenth century, it is still, in all probability, the most important fact in the faith and conduct of the race, running with endless applications throughout the spheres of practical life and vibrating away to the extremities of the imagi-nation. In the case of this poor, devout, high-minded

James Lane Allen

Kentucky boy, at work on a farm in the years 1866 and 1867, saving his earnings and reading his Bible as the twofold preparation for his entrance into the Christian ministry, this belief took on one of its purest shapes and wrought out in him some of its loftiest results.

Let it be remembered that he lived in a temperate, beautiful, bountiful country; that his work was done mostly in the fields, with the aspects of land and sky ever before him; that he was much alone; that his thinking was nearly always of his Bible and his Bible college. Let it be remembered that he had an eye which was not merely an opening and closing but a seeing eye - full of health and of enjoyment of the pageantry of things; and that behind this eye, looking through it as through its window, stood the dim soul of the lad, itself in a temple of perpetual worship: these are some of the conditions which yielded him during these two years the intense, exalted realities of his inner life.

When of morning he stepped out of the plain farm-house with its rotting doors and leaking roof and started off joyously to his day's work, at the sight of the great sun just rising above the low dew-wet hills, his soul would go soaring away to heaven's gate. Sometimes he would be abroad late at night, summoning the doctor for his father or returning from a visit to another neighborhood. In every farmhouse that he passed on the country road the people were asleep - over all the shadowy land they were asleep. And everywhere, guardian in the darkness, watched the moon, pouring its searching beams upon every roof, around every entrance, on kennel and fold, sty and barn - with light not enough to awaken but enough to protect: how he worshipped toward that lamp tended by the Sleepless! There were summer noons when he would be lying under a solitary tree in a field - in the edge of its shade, resting; his face turned toward the sky. This would be one over-bending vault of serenest blue, save for a distant flight of snow-white clouds, making him think of some earthward-wandering company of angels. He would lie motionless, scarce breathing, in that peace of the earth, that smile of the Father. Or if this same vault remained serene too long; if the soil of the fields became dusty to his boots and his young grain began to wither, when at last, in response to his prayer, the clouds were brought directly over them and emptied down, as he stepped forth into the cooled, dripping, soaking green, how his heart blessed the Power that reigned above and did all things well!

It was always praise, gratitude, thanks-giving, what-ever happened. If he prayed for rain for his crops and none was sent, then he thought his prayer lacked faith or was unwise, he knew not how; if too much rain fell, so that his grain rotted, this again was from some fault of his or for his good; or perhaps it was the evil work of the prince of the powers of the air - by permission of the Omnipotent. In the case of one crop all the labor of nearly a year went for nothing: he explained this as a reminder that he must be chastened.

Come good, come ill, then, crops or no crops, increase or decrease, it was all the same to him: he traced the cause of all plenty as of all disappointment and disaster reaching him through the laws of nature to some benevolent purpose of the Ruler. And ever before his eyes also he kept that spotless Figure which once walked among men on earth - that Saviour of the world whose service he was soon to enter, whose words of everlasting life he was to preach: his father's farm

James Lane Allen

became as the vineyard of the parables in the Gospels, he a laborer in it.

Thus this lad was nearer the first century and yet earlier ages than the nineteenth. He knew more of prophets and apostles than modern doctors of divinity. When the long-looked-for day arrived for him to throw his arms around his father and mother and bid them good-by, he should have mounted a camel, like a youth of the Holy Land of old, and taken his solemn, tender way across the country toward Jerusalem.

V

One crisp, autumn morning, then, of that year 1867, a big, raw-boned, bashful lad, having passed at the turnstile into the twenty-acre campus, stood reverently still before the majestical front of Morrison College. Browned by heat and wind, rain and sun; straight of spine, fine of nerve, tough of muscle. In one hand he carried an enormous, faded valise, made of Brussels carpet copiously sprinkled with small, pink roses; in the other, held like a horizontal javelin, a family umbrella. A broken rib escaped his fingers.

It was no time and place for observation or emotion. The turnstile behind him was kept in a whirl by students pushing through and hurrying toward the college a few hundred yards distant; others, who had just left it, came tramping toward him and passing out. In a retired part of the campus, he could see several pacing slowly to and fro in the grass, holding text-books before their faces. Some were grouped at the bases of the big Doric columns, at work together. From behind the college on the right, two or three appeared running and disappeared through a basement entrance. Out of the grass somewhere came the sound of a whistle as clear and happy as of a quail in the wheat; from another direction, the shouts and wrangling of a playground. Once, barely audible, through the air surged and died away the last bars of a glorious hymn, sung by a chorus of fresh male voices. The whole scene was one of bustle, work, sport, worship.

A few moments the lad remained where he had halted, drinking through every thirsting pore; but most of all with his eyes satisfied by the sight of that venerable building which, morning and night, for over two years had shaped itself to his imagination - that seat of the university - that entrance into his future.

Three students came strolling along the path toward him on their way down town. One was slapping his book against his thigh; one was blowing a ditty through his nose, like music on a comb; one, in the middle, had his arms thrown over the shoulders of the others, and was at intervals using them as crutches. As they were about to pass the lad, who had stepped a few feet to one side of the path, they wheeled and laughed at him.

"Hello, preachy!" cried one. His face was round, red, and soft, like the full moon; the disk was now broken up by smiling creases.

"Can you tell me," inquired the lad, coloring and wondering how it was already known that he was to be a preacher, "Can you tell me just the way to the Bible College?"

The one of the three on the right turned to the middle man and repeated the question gravely: -

"Can you tell me just the way to the Bible College?"

The middle man turned and repeated it gravely to the one on the left: -

"Can you tell me just the way to the Bible College?"

The one on the left seized a passing student: -

"Can you tell us all just the way to the Bible College?"

"Ministers of grace!" he said, "without the angels!" Then turning to the lad, he continued: "You see this path? Take it! Those steps? Go straight up those steps. Those doors? Enter! Then, if you don't see the Bible College, maybe you'll see the janitor - if he is there. But don't you fear! You may get lost, but you'll never get away!"

The lad knew he was being guyed, but he didn't mind: what hurt him was that his Bible College should be treated with such levity.

"Thank you," he said pleasantly but proudly.

"Have you matriculated?" one of the three called after him as he started forward.

David had never heard that word; but he entertained such a respect for knowledge that he hated to appear unnecessarily ignorant.

"I don't think - I have," he observed vaguely.

The small eyes of the full moon disappeared altogether this time.

"Well, you've got to matriculate, you know," he said. "You'd better do that sometime. But don't speak of it to your professors, or to anybody connected with the college. It must be kept secret."

"Will I be too late for the first recitations?"

The eager question was on the lad's lips but never uttered. The trio had wheeled carelessly away.

There passed them, coming toward David, a tall, gaunt, rough-whiskered man, wearing a paper collar without a cravat, and a shiny, long-tailed, black cloth coat. He held a Bible opened at Genesis.

"Good morning, brother," he said frankly, speaking in the simple kindness which comes from being a husband and father. "You are going to enter the Bible College, I see."

"Yes, sir," replied the lad. "Are you one of the professors?"

The middle-aged man laughed painfully.

"I am one of the students."

David felt that he had inflicted a wound. "How many students are here?" he asked quickly.

"About a thousand."

The two walked side by side toward the college.

"Have you matriculated?" inquired the lad's companion. There was that awful word again!

"I don't know HOW to matriculate. How DO you matriculate? What is matriculating?"

"I'LL go with you. I'LL show you," said the simple

fatherly guide.

"Thank you, if you will" breathed the lad, gratefully.

After a brief silence his companion spoke again.

"I'm late in life in entering college. I've got a son half as big as you and a baby; and my wife's here. But, you see, I've had a hard time. I've preached for years. But I wasn't satisfied. I wanted to understand the Bible better. And this is the place to do that." Now that he had explained himself, he looked relieved.

"Well," said David, fervently, entering at once into a brotherhood with this kindly soul, "that's what I've come for, too. I want to understand the Bible better - and if I am ever worthy - I want to preach it. And you have baptized people already?"

"Hundreds of them. Here we are," said his companion, as they passed under a low doorway, on one side of the pillared steps.

"Here I am at last," repeated the lad to himself with solemn joy, "And now God be with me!"

By the end of that week he had the run of things; had met his professors, one of whom had preached that sermon two summers before, and now, on being told who the lad was, welcomed him as a sheaf out of that sowing; had been assigned to his classes; had gone down town to the little packed and crowded book-store and bought the needful student's supplies - so making the first draught on his money; been assigned to a poor room in the austere dormitory behind the college; made his first failures in recitations, standing before his professor with no more articulate voice and no more courage than a sheep; and had awakened to a new sense - the brotherhood of young souls about him, the men of his college.

A revelation they were! Nearly all poor like himself; nearly all having worked their way to the university: some from farms, some by teaching distant country or mountain schools; some by the peddling of books - out of unknown byways, from the hedges and ditches of life, they had assembled: Calvary's regulars.

One scene in his new life struck upon the lad's imagination like a vision out of the New Testament, - his first supper in the bare dining room of that dormitory: the single long, rough table; the coarse, frugal food; the shadows of the evening hour; at every chair a form reverently standing; the saying of the brief grace - ah, that first supper with the disciples!

Among the things he had to describe in his letter to his father and mother, this scene came last; and his final words to them were a blessing that they had made him one of this company of young men.

VI

The lad could not study eternally. The change from a toiling body and idle mind to an idle body and toiling mind requires time to make the latter condition unirksome. Happily there was small need to delve at learning. His brain was like that of a healthy wild animal freshly captured from nature. And as such an animal learns to snap at flung bits of food, springing to meet them and sinking back on his haunches keen-eyed for more; so mentally he caught at the lessons prepared for him by his professors: every faculty asked only to be fed - and remained hungry after the feeding.

Of afternoons, therefore, when recitations were over and his muscles ached for exercise, he donned his old farm hat and went, stepping in his high, awkward, investigating way around the town - unaware of himself, unaware of the light-minded who often turned to smile at that great gawk in grotesque garments, with his face full of beatitudes and his pockets full of apples. For apples were beginning to come in from the frosty orchards; and the fruit dealers along the streets piled them into pyramids of temptation. It seemed a hardship to him to have to spend priceless money for a thing like apples, which had always been as cheap and plentiful as spring water. But those evening suppers in the dormitory with the disciples! Even when he was filled (which was not often) he was never comforted;

and one day happening upon one of those pomological pyramids, he paused, yearned, and bought the apex. It was harder not to buy than to buy. After that he fell into this fruitful vice almost diurnally; and with mortifying worldly-mindedness he would sometimes find his thoughts straying apple-wards while his professors were personally conducting him through Canaan or leading him dry-shod across the Red Sea. The little dealer soon learned to anticipate his approach; and as he drew up would have the requisite number ready and slide them into his pockets without a word - and without the chance of inspection. A man's candy famine attacked him also. He usually bought some intractable, resisting medium: it left him rather tired of pleasure.

So during those crude days he went strolling solemnly about the town, eating, exploring, filling with sweet-meats and filled with wonder. It was the first city he had ever seen, the chief interior city of the state. From childhood he had longed to visit it. The thronged streets, the curious stores, the splendid residences, the flashing equipages - what a new world it was to him! But the first place he inquired his way to was the factory where he had sold his hemp. Awhile he watched the men at work, wondering whether they might not then be handling some that he had broken.

At an early date also he went to look up his dear old neighborhood schoolfellows who two years before had left him, to enter another college of the University. By inquiry he found out where they lived - in a big, handsome boarding-house on a fashionable street. He thought he had never even dreamed of anything so fine as was this house - nor had he. As he sat in the rich parlors, waiting to learn whether his friends were at home, he glanced uneasily at his shoes to see whether they might not be soiling the carpet; and he vigorously dusted himself with his breath and hands - thus depositing on the furniture whatever dust there was to transfer.

Having been invited to come up to his friends' room, he mounted and found one of them waiting at the head of the stairs in his shirt sleeves, smoking. His greeting was hearty in its way yet betokened some surprise, a little uneasiness, condescension. David followed his host into a magnificent room with enormous windows, now raised and opening upon a veranda. Below was a garden full of old vines black with grapes and pear trees bent down with pears and beds bright with cool autumn flowers. (The lad made a note of how much money he would save on apples if he could only live in reach of those pear trees.) There was a big rumpled bed in the room; and stretched across this bed on his stomach lay a student studying and waving his heels slowly in the air. A table stood in the middle of the room: the books and papers had been scraped off to the floor; four students were seated at it playing cards and smoking. Among them his other friend, who rose and gave him a hearty grip and resuming his seat asked what was trumps. A voice he had heard before called out to him from the table: -

"Hello, preachy! Did you find your way to the Bible College?"

Whereupon the student on the bed rolled heavily over, sat up dejectedly, and ogled him with red eyes and a sagging jaw.

"Have you matriculated?" he asked.

David did not think of the cards, and he liked the greeting of the two strangers who guyed him better than the welcome of his old friends. That hurt: he had never supposed there was anything just like it in the nature of man. But during the years since he had seen them, old times were gone, old manners changed. And was it not in the hemp fields of the father of one of them that he had meantime worked with the negroes? And is there any other country in the world where the clean laborer is so theoretically honored and so practically despised as by the American snob of each sex?

One afternoon he went over to the courthouse and got the county clerk to show him the entry where his great-grandfather had had the deed to his church recorded. There it all was! - all written down to hold good while the world lasted: that perpetual grant of part and parcel of his land, for the use of a free school and a free church. The lad went reverently over the plain, rough speech of the mighty old pioneer, as he spoke out his purpose.

During those early days also he sought out the different churches, scrutinizing respectfully their exteriors. How many they were, and how grand nearly all! Beyond anything he had imagined. He reasoned that if the buildings were so fine, how fine must be the singing and the sermons! The unconscious assumption, the false logic here, was creditable to his heart at least - to that green trust of the young in things as they should be which becomes in time the best seasoned staff of age. He hunted out especially the Catholic Church. His great-grandfather had founded his as free for Catholics as Protestants, but he recalled the fact that no priest had ever preached there. He felt very curious to see a priest. A synagogue in the town he could not find. He was sorry. He had a great desire to lay eyes on a synagogue - temple of that ancient faith which had flowed on its deep way across the centuries without a ripple of disturbance from the Christ. He had made up his mind that when he began to preach he would often preach especially to the Jews: the time perhaps had come when the Father, their Father, would reveal his Son to them also. Thus he promptly fixed in mind the sites of all the churches, because he intended in time to go to them all.

Meantime he attended his own, the size and elegance of which were a marvel; and in it especially the red velvet pulpit and the vast chandelier (he had never seen a chandelier before), blazing with stars (he had never seen illuminating gas). It was under this chandelier that he himself soon found a seat. All the Bible students sat there who could get there, that being the choir of male voices; and before a month passed he had been taken into this choir: for a storm-like bass rolled out of him as easily as thunder out of a June cloud. Thus uneventful flowed the tenor of his student life during those several initiatory weeks: then something occurred that began to make grave history for him.

The pastor announced at service one morning that he would that day begin a series of sermons on errors in the faith and practice of the different Protestant sects; though he would also consider in time the cases of the Catholics and Jews: it would scarcely be necessary to speak of the Mohammedans and such others. He was driven to do this, he declared, and was anxious to do it, as part of the work of his brethren all over the country; which was the restoration of Apostolic Christianity to the world. He asked the especial attention of the Bible students of the University to these sermons: the first of which he then proceeded to preach.

That night the lad was absent from his place: he was seated in the church which had been riddled with logic in the morning. Just why it would be hard to say. Perhaps his motive resembled that which prompts us to visit a battle-field and count the slain. Only, not a soul of those people seemed even to have been wounded. They sang, prayed, preached, demeaned themselves generally as those who believed that THEY were the express chosen of the Lord, and greatly enjoyed the notorious fact.

The series of sermons went on: every night the lad was missing from his place - gone to see for himself and to learn more about those worldly churches which had departed from the faith once delivered to the saints, and if saved at all, then by the mercy of God and much of it.

In the history of any human soul it is impossible to grasp the first event that starts up a revolution. But perhaps the troubles of the lad began here. His absences from Sunday night service of course attracted notice under the chandelier. His bass was missed. Another student was glad to take his place. His roommate and the several other dormitory students who had become his acquaintances, discussed with him the impropriety of these absences: they agreed that he would better stick to his own church. He gave reasons why he should follow up the pastor's demonstrations with actual visits to the others: he contended that the pastor established the fact of the errors; but that the best way to understand any error was to study the erring. This was all new to him, however. He had not supposed that in educating himself to preach the simple Gospel, to the end that the world might believe in Christ, he must also preach against those who believed in Christ already. Besides, no one seemed to be convinced by the pastor but those who agreed with him in advance: the other churches flourished quite the same.

He cited a sermon he had heard in one, which, to the satisfaction of all present, had riddled his own church, every word of the proof being based on Scripture: so there you were!

A little cloud came that instant between David and the students to whom he expressed these views. Some rejoined hotly at once; some maintained the cold silence which intends to speak in its own time. The next thing the lad knew was that a professor requested him to remain after class one day; and speaking with grave kindness, advised him to go regularly to his own church thereafter. The lad entered ardently into the reasons why he had gone to the others. The professor heard him through and without comment repeated his grave, kind advice.

Thereafter the lad was regularly in his own seat there - but with a certain mysterious, beautiful feeling gone. He could not have said what this feeling was, did not himself know. Only, a slight film seemed to pass before his eyes when he looked at his professor, so that he saw him less clearly and as more remote.

One morning there was a sermon on the Catholics. David went dutifully to his professor. He said he had never been to a Catholic Church and would like to go. His professor assented cordially, evincing his pleasure in the lad's frankness. But the next Sunday morning he was in the Catholic Church again, thus for the first time missing the communion in his own. Of all the congregations of Christian believers that the lad had now visited, the Catholic impressed him as being the most solemn, reverent, and best mannered. In his own church the place did not seem to become the house of God till services began; and one morning in particular, two old farmers in the pew behind him talked in smothered tones of stock and crops, till it fairly made him homesick. The sermon of the priest, too, filled him with amazement. It weighed the claims of various Protestant sects to be reckoned as parts of the one true historic church of God. In passing, he barely referred to the most modern of these self-constituted Protestant bodies - David's own church - and dismissed it with one blast of scorn, which seemed to strike the lad's face like a hot wind: it left it burning. But to the Episcopal Church the priest dispensed the most vitriolic criticism. And that night, carried away by the old impulse, which had grown now almost into a habit, David went to the Episcopal Church: went to number the slain. The Bishop of the diocese, as it happened, was preaching that night - preaching on the union of Christian believers. He showed how ready the Episcopal Church was for such a union if the rest would only consent: but no other church, he averred, must expect the Episcopal Church ever to surrender one article of its creed, namely: that it alone was descended not by historical continuity simply, but by Divine succession from the Apostles themselves. The lad walked slowly back to the dormitory that night with knit brows and a heavy heart.

A great change was coming over him. His old religious peace had been unexpectedly disturbed. He found himself in the thick of the wars of dogmatic theology. At that time and in that part of the United States these were impassioned and rancorous to a degree which even now, less than half a century later, can scarce be understood; so rapidly has developed meantime that modern spirit which is for us the tolerant transition to a yet broader future. Had Kentucky been peopled by her same people several generations earlier, the land would have run red with the blood of religious persecutions, as never were England and Scotland at their worst. So that this lad, brought in from his solemn, cloistered fields and introduced to wrangling, sarcastic, envious creeds, had already begun to feel doubtful and distressed, not knowing what to believe nor whom to follow. He had commenced by being so plastic a medium for faith, that he had tried to believe them all. Now he was in the intermediate state of trying to ascertain which. From that state there are two and two only final ones to emerge: "I shall among them believe this one only;" or, "I shall among them believe - none." The constant discussion of some dogma and disproof of some dogma inevitably begets in a certain order of mind the temper to discuss and distrust ALL dogma.

Not over their theologies alone were the churches wrangling before the lad's distracted thoughts. If the theologies were rending religion, politics was rending the theologies. The war just ended had not brought, as the summer sermon of the Bible College professor had stated, breadth of mind for narrowness, calm for passion. Not while men are fighting their wars of conscience do they hate most, but after they have fought; and Southern and Union now hated to the bottom and nowhere else as at their prayers. David found a Presbyterian Church on one street called "Southern" and one a few blocks away called

"Northern": how those brethren dwelt together. The Methodists were similarly divided. Of Baptists, the lad ascertained there had been so many kinds and parts of kinds since the settlement of Kentucky, that apparently any large-sized family anywhere could reasonably have constituted itself a church, if the parents and children had only been fortunate enough to agree.

Where politics did not cleave, other issues did. The Episcopal Church was cleft into a reform movement (and one unreformable). In his own denomination internal discord raged over such questions as diabolic pleasures and Apostolic music. He saw young people haled before the pulpit as before a tribunal of exact statutes and expelled for moving their feet in certain ways. If in dancing they whirled like a top instead of being shot straight back and forth like a bobbin in a weaver's shuttle, their moral conduct was aggravated. A church organ was ridiculed as a sort of musical Behemoth - as a dark chamber of howling, roaring Belial.

These controversies overflowed from the congregation to the Bible College. The lad in his room at the dormitory one Sunday afternoon heard a debate on whether a tuning fork is a violation of the word of God. The debaters turned to him excited and angry: -

"What do you think?" they asked.

"I don't think it is worth talking about," he replied quietly.

They soon became reconciled to each other; they never forgave him.

Meantime as for his Biblical studies, they enlarged enormously his knowledge of the Bible; but they added enormously to the questions that may be asked about the Bible - questions he had never thought of before. And in adding to the questions that may be asked, they multiplied those that cannot be answered. The lad began to ask these questions, began to get no answers. The ground of his interest in the great Book shifted. Out on the farm alone with it for two years, reading it never with a critical but always with a worshipping mind, it had been to him simply the summons to a great and good life, earthly and immortal. As he sat in the lecture rooms, studying it book by book, paragraph by paragraph, writing chalk notes about it on the blackboard, hearing the students recite it as they recited arithmetic or rhetoric, a little homesickness overcame him for the hours when he had read it at the end of a furrow in the fields, or by his candle the last thing at night before he kneeled to say his prayers, or of Sunday afternoons off by himself in the sacred leafy woods. The mysterious untouched Christ-feeling was in him so strong, that he shrank from these critical analyses as he would from dissecting the body of the crucified Redeemer.

A significant occurrence took place one afternoon some seven months after he had entered the University.

On that day, recitations over, the lad left the college alone and with a most thoughtful air crossed the campus and took his course into the city. Reaching a great central street, he turned to the left and proceeded until he stood opposite a large brick church. Passing along the outside of this, he descended a few steps, traversed an alley, knocked timidly at a door, and by a voice within was bidden to enter. He did so, and stood in his pastor's study. He had told his pastor that he would like to have a little talk with him, and the pastor was there to have the little talk.

During those seven months the lad had been attracting notice more and more. The Bible students had cast up his reckoning unfavorably: he was not of their kind - they moved through their studies as one flock of sheep through a valley, drinking the same water, nipping the same grass, and finding it what they wanted. His professors had singled him out as a case needing peculiar guidance. Not in his decorum as a student: he was the very soul of discipline. Not in slackness of study: his mind consumed knowledge as a flame tinder. Not in any irregularities of private life: his morals were as snow for whiteness. Yet none other caused such concern.

All this the pastor knew; he had himself long had his eye on this lad. During his sermons, among the rows of heads and brows and eyes upturned to him, oftenest he felt himself looking at that big shock-head, at those grave brows, into those eager, troubled eyes. His persistent demonstrations that he and his brethren alone were right and all other churches Scripturally wrong - they always seemed to take the light out of that countenance. There was silence in the study now as the lad modestly seated himself in a chair which the pastor had pointed out.

After fidgeting a few moments, he addressed the logician with a stupefying premise: -

"My great-grandfather," he said, "once built a church simply to God, not to any man's opinions of Him."

He broke off abruptly.

"So did Voltaire," remarked the pastor dryly, coming to the rescue. "Voltaire built a church to God: 'Erexit deo Voltaire' Your great-grandfather and Voltaire must have been kin to each other."

The lad had never heard of Voltaire. The information was rather prepossessing.

"I think I should admire Voltaire," he observed reflectively.

"So did the Devil," remarked the pastor. Then he added pleasantly, for he had a Scotch relish for a theological jest: -

"You may meet Voltaire some day."

"I should like to. Is he coming here?" asked the lad.

"Not immediately. He is in hell - or will be after the Resurrection of the Dead."

The silence in the study grew intense.

"I understand you now," said the lad, speaking composedly all at once. "You think that perhaps I will go to the Devil also."

"Oh, no!" exclaimed the pastor, hiding his smile and stroking his beard with syllogistic self-respect. "My dear young brother, did you want to see me on any - BUSINESS?"

"I did. I was trying to tell you. My great-grandfather - "

"Couldn't you begin with more modern times?"

"The story begins back there," insisted the lad, firmly. "The part of it, at least, that affects me. My great-grandfather founded a church free to all Christian believers. It stands in our neighborhood. I have always gone there. I joined the church there. All the different denominations in our part of the country have held services there. Sometimes they have all had services together. I grew up to think they were all equally good Christians in their different ways."

"Did you?" inquired the pastor. "You and your grandfather and Voltaire must ALL be kin to each other."

His visage was not pleasant.

"My trouble since coming to College," said the lad, pressing across the interruption, "has been to know which IS the right church - "

"Are you a member of THIS church?" inquired the pastor sharply, calling a halt to this folly.

"I am."

"Then don't you know that it is the only right one?"

"I do not. All the others declare it a wrong one. They stand ready to prove this by the Scriptures and do prove it to their satisfaction. They declare that if I become a preacher of what my church believes, I shall become a false teacher of men and be responsible to God for the souls I may lead astray. They honestly believe this."

"Don't you know that when Satan has entered into a man, he can make him honestly believe anything?"

"And you think it is Satan that keeps the other churches from seeing this is the only right one?"

"I do! And beware, young man, that Satan does not get into YOU"

"He must be in me already." There was silence again, then the lad continued.

"All this is becoming a great trouble to me. It interferes with my studies - takes my interest out of my future. I come to you then. You are my pastor. Where is the truth - the reason - the proof - the authority? Where is the guiding LAW in all this? I must find THE LAW and that quickly."

There was no gainsaying his trouble: it expressed itself in his eyes, voice, entire demeanor. The pastor was not seeing any of these things. Here was a plain, ignorant country lad who had rejected his logic and who apparently had not tact enough at this moment to appreciate his own effrontery. In the whole sensitive-ness of man there is no spot so touchy as the theological.

"Have you a copy of the New Testament?"

It was the tone in which the school-master of old times said, "Bring me that switch."

"I have,"

"You can read it?"

"I can."

"You find in it the inspired account of the faith of the original church - the earliest history of Apostolic Christianity?"

"I do."

"Then, can you not compare the teachings of the Apostles, THEIR faith and THEIR practice, with the teachings of this church? ITS faith and ITS practice?"

"I have tried to do that"

"Then there is the truth. And the reason. And the proof. And the authority. And the LAW. We have no creed but the creed of the Apostolic churches; no practice but their practice; no teaching but their teaching in letter and in spirit."

"That is what was told me before I came to college. It was told me that young men were to be prepared to preach the simple Gospel of Christ to all the world. There was to be no sectarian theology."

"Well? Has any one taught you sectarian theology?"

"Not consciously, not intentionally. Inevitably - perhaps. That is my trouble now - ONE of my troubles."

"Well?"

"May I ask you some questions?"

"You may ask me some questions if they are not silly

questions. You don't seem to have any creed, but you DO seem to have a catechism! Well, on with the catechism! I hope it will be better than those I have read."

So bidden, the lad began; -

"Is it Apostolic Christianity to declare that infants should not be baptized?"

"It is!" The reply came like a flash of lightning.

"And those who teach to the contrary violate the word of God?"

"They do!"

"Is it Apostolic Christianity to affirm that only immersion is Christian baptism?"

"It is!"

"And those who use any other form violate the word of God?"

"They do!"

"Is it Apostolic Christianity to celebrate the Lord's Supper once every seven days?"

"It is!"

"And all who observe a different custom violate the word of God?"

"They do!"

"Is it Apostolic Christianity to have no such officer in the church as an Episcopal bishop?"

"It is!"

"The office of Bishop, then, is a violation of Apostolic Christianity?"

"It is!"

"Is it Apostolic Christianity to make every congregation, no matter how small or influenced by passion, an absolute court of trial and punishment of his members?"

"It is!"

"To give every such body control over the religious standing of its members, so it may turn them out into the world, banish them from the church of Christ forever, if it sees fit?"

"It is!"

"And those who frame any other system of church government violate the - "

"They do!"

"Is it Apostolic Christianity to teach that faith precedes repentance?"

"It is!"

"Those who teach that sorrow for sin is itself the great reason why we believe in Christ - do they violate - ?"

"They do!"

"Is it Apostolic Christianity to turn people out of the church for dancing?"

"It is!"

"The use of an organ in worship - is that a violation of Apostolic - ?"

"It is!"

"Is it Apostolic Christianity to require that the believer in it shall likewise believe everything in the old Bible?"

"It is."

"Did Christ and the Apostles themselves teach that everything contained in what we call the old Bible must be believed?"

"They did!"

The pastor was grasping the arms of his chair, his body bent toward the lad, his head thrown back, his face livid with sacred rage. He was a good man, tried and true: God-fearing, God-serving. No fault lay in him unless it may be imputed for unrighteousness that he was a stanch, trenchant sectary in his place and generation. As he sat there in the basement study of his church, his pulpit of authority and his baptismal pool of regeneration directly over his head, all round him in the city the solid hundreds of his followers, he forgot himself as a man and a minister and remembered only that as a servant of the Most High he was being interrogated and dishonored. His soul shook and thundered within him to repel these attacks upon his Lord and Master. As those unexpected random questions had poured in upon him thick and fast, all emerging, as it seemed to him, like disembodied evil spirits from the black pit of Satan and the damned, it was joy to him to deal to each that same straight,

God-directed spear-thrust of a reply - killing them as they rose. His soul exulted in that blessed carnage.

But the questions ceased. They had hurried out as though there were a myriad pressing behind - a few issuing bees of an aroused swarm. But they ceased. The pastor leaned back in his chair and drew a quivering breath through his white lips.

"Ask some more!"

On his side, the lad had lost divine passion as the pastor had gained it. His interest waned while the pastor's waxed. His last questions were put so falteringly, almost so inaudibly, that the pastor might well believe his questioner beaten, brought back to modesty and silence. To a deeper-seeing eye, however, the truth would have been plain that the lad was not seeing his pastor at all, but seeing THROUGH him into his own future: into his life, his great chosen life-work. His young feet had come in their travels nigh to the limits of his Promised Land: he was looking over into it.

"Ask some more! The last of them! Out with them ALL! Make an end of this now and here!"

The lad reached for his hat, which he had laid on the

floor, and stood up. He was as pale as the dead.

"I shall never be able to preach Apostolic Christianity," he said, and turned to the door.

But reaching it, he wheeled and came back.

"I am in trouble!" he cried, sitting down again. "I don't know what to believe. I don't know what I do believe. My God!" he cried again, burying his face in his hands. "I believe I am beginning to doubt the Bible. Great God, what am I coming to! what is my life coming to! ME doubt the Bible!". . .

The interview of that day was one of the signs of two storms which were approaching: one appointed to reach the University, one to reach the lad.

The storm now gathering in many quarters and destined in a few years to burst upon the University was like its other storms that had gone before: only, this last one left it a ruin which will stay a ruin.

That oldest, best passion of the Kentucky people for the establishment in their own land of a broad institution of learning for their own sons, though revived in David's time on a greater scale than ever before, was not to be realized. The new University, bearing the name of the commonwealth and opening at the close of the Civil War as a sign of the new peace of the new nation, having begun so fairly and risen in a few years to fourth or fifth place in patronage among all those in the land, was already entering upon its decline. The reasons of this were the same that had successively ruined each of its predecessors: the same old sectarian quarrels, enmities, revenges; the same old political oppositions and hatreds; the same personal ambitions, jealousies, strifes.

Away back in 1780, while every man, woman, and child in the western wilderness ness was in dire struggle for life itself, those far-seeing people had induced the General Assembly of Virginia to confiscate and sell in Kentucky the lands of British Tories, to found a public seminary for Kentucky boys - not a sectarian school. These same broad-minded pioneers had later persuaded her to give twenty thousand acres of her land to the same cause and to exempt officers and students of the institution from military service. Still later, intent upon this great work, they had induced Virginia to take from her own beloved William and Mary one-sixth of all surveyors' fees in the district and contribute them. The early Kentuckians, for their part, planned and sold out a lottery - to help along the incorruptible work. For such an institution Washington and Adams and Aaron Burr and Thomas Marshall and many another opened their purses. For it thousands and thousands of dollars were raised among friends scattered throughout the Atlantic states, these responding to a petition addressed to all religious sects, to all political parties. A library and philosophical apparatus were wagoned over the Alleghanies. A committee was sent to England to choose further equipments. When Kentucky came to have a legislature of its own, it decreed that each of the counties in the state should receive six thousand acres of land wherewith to start a seminary; and that all these county seminaries were to train students for this long-dreamed-of central institution. That they might not be sent away - to the North or to Europe. When, at the end of the Civil War, a fresh attempt (and the last) was made to found in reality and in perpetuity a home institution to be as good as the best in the republic, the people rallied as though they had never known defeat. The idea resounded like a great trumpet throughout the land. Individual, legislative, congressional aid - all were poured out lavishly for that one devoted cause.

Sad chapter in the history of the Kentuckians! Perhaps the saddest among the many sad ones.

For such an institution must in time have taught what all its court-houses and all its pulpits - laws human and divine - have not been able to teach: it must have taught the noble commonwealth to cease murdering. Standing there in the heart of the people's land, it must have grown to stand in the heart of their affections: and so standing, to stand for peace. For true learning always stands for peace. Letters always stand for peace. And it is the scholar of the world who has ever come into it as Christ came: to teach that human life is worth saving and must be saved.

VII

The storm approaching David was vaster and came faster.

Several days had passed since his anxious and abruptly terminated interview with his pastor. During the interval he had addressed no further inquiries to any man touching his religious doubts. A serious sign: for when we cease to carry such burdens to those who wait near by as our recognized counsellors and appointed guides, the inference is that succor for our peculiar need has there been sought in vain. This succor, if existent at all, will be found elsewhere in one of two places: either farther away from home in greater minds whose teaching has not yet reached us; or still nearer home in what remains as the last court of inquiry and decision: in the mind itself. With greater intellects more remote the lad had not yet been put in touch; he had therefore grown reflective, and for nearly a week had been spending the best powers of his unaided thought in self-examination.

He was sitting one morning at his student's table with his Bible and note-book opened before him, wrestling with his problems still. The dormitory was very quiet. A few students remained indoors at work, but most were absent: some gone into the country to preach trial sermons to trying congregations; some down in the town; some at the college, practising hymns, or rehearsing for society exhibitions; some scattered over the campus, preparing Monday lessons on a spring morning when animal sap stirs intelligently at its sources and sends up its mingled currents of new energy and new lassitude.

David had thrown his window wide open, to let in the fine air; his eyes strayed outward. A few yards away stood a stunted transplanted locust - one of those uncomplaining asses of the vegetable kingdom whose mission in life is to carry whatever man imposes. Year after year this particular tree had remained patiently backed up behind the dormitory, for the bearing of garments to be dusted or dried. More than once during the winter, the lad had gazed out of his snow-crusted panes at this dwarfed donkey of the woods, its feet buried deep in ashes, its body covered with kitchen wash-rags and Bible students' frozen underwear. He had reasoned that such soil and such servitude had killed it.

But as he looked out of his window now, his eyes caught sight of the early faltering green in which this exile of the forest was still struggling to clothe itself - its own life vestments. Its enforced and artificial function as a human clothes-horse had indeed nearly destroyed it; but wherever a bud survived, there its true office in nature was asserted, its ancient kind declared, its growth stubbornly resumed.

The moment for the lad may have been one of those in the development of the young when they suddenly behold familiar objects as with eyes more clearly opened; when the neutral becomes the decisive; when the sermon is found in the stone. As he now took

James Lane Allen

curious cognizance of the budding wood which he, seeing it only in winter, had supposed could not bud again, he fell to marvelling how constant each separate thing in nature is to its own life and how sole is its obligation to live that life only. All that a locust had to do in the world was to be a locust; and be a locust it would though it perished in the attempt. It drew back with no hesitation, was racked with no doubt, puzzled with no necessity of preference. It knew absolutely the law of its own being and knew absolutely nothing else; found under that law its liberty, found under that liberty its life.

"But I," he reflected, "am that which was never sown and never grown before. All the ages of time, all the generations of men, have not fixed any type of life for me. What I am to become I must myself each instant choose; and having chosen, I can never know that I have chosen best. Often I do know that what I have selected I must discard. And yet no one choice can ever be replaced by its rejected fellow; the better chance lost once, is lost eternally. Within the limits of a locust, how little may the individual wander; within the limits of the wide and erring human, what may not a man become! What now am I becoming? What shall I now choose - as my second choice?"

A certain homely parallel between the tree and himself began to shape itself before his thought: how he, too, had been dug up far away - had, in a sense, voluntarily dug himself up - and been transplanted in the college campus; how, ever since being placed there, the different sectarian churches of the town had, without exception, begun to pin on the branches of his mind the many-shaped garments of their dogmas, until by this time he appeared to himself as completely draped as the little locust after a heavy dormitory washing. There was this terrible difference, however: that the garments hung on the tree were anon removed; but these doctrines and dogmas were fastened to his mind to stay - as the very foliage of his thought - as the living leaves of Divine Truth. He was forbidden to strip off one of those sacred leaves. He was told to live and to breathe his religious life through them, and to grow only where they hung.

The lad declared finally to himself this morning, that realize his religious life through those dogmas he never could; that it was useless any longer to try. Little by little they would as certainly kill him in growth and spirit as the rags had killed the locust in sap and bud. Whatever they might be to others - and he judged no man - for him with his peculiar nature they could never be life-vestments; they would become his spiritual grave-clothes.

The parallel went a little way further: that scant faltering green! that unconquerable effort of the tree to assert despite all deadening experiences its old wildwood state! Could he do the like, could he go back to his? Yearning, sad, immeasurable filled him as he now recalled the simple faith of what had already seemed to him his childhood. Through the mist blinding his vision, through the doubts blinding his brain, still could he see it lying there clear in the near distance! "No," he cried, "into whatsoever future I may be driven to enter, closed against me is the peace of my past. Return thither my eyes ever will, my feet never!"

"But as I was true to myself then, let me be true now. If I cannot believe what I formerly believed, let me determine quickly what I CAN believe. The Truth, the

James Lane Allen

Law - I must find these and quickly!"

From all of which, though thus obscurely set forth, it will be divined that the lad had now reached, indeed for some days had stood halting, at one of the great partings of the ways: when the whole of Life's road can be walked in by us no longer; when we must elect the half we shall henceforth follow, and having taken it, ever afterward perhaps look yearningly back upon the other as a lost trail of the mind.

The parting of the ways where he had thus faltered, summing up his bewilderment, and crying aloud for fresh directions, was one immemorially old in the history of man: the splitting of Life's single road into the by-paths of Doubt and Faith. Until within less than a year, his entire youth had been passed in the possession of what he esteemed true religion. Brought from the country into the town, where each of the many churches was proclaiming itself the sole incarnation of this and all others the embodiment of something false, he had, after months of distracted wandering among their contradictory clamors, passed as so many have passed before him into that state of mind which rejects them all and asks whether such a thing as true religion anywhere exists.

The parting of Life's road at Doubt and Faith! How many pilgrim feet throughout the ages, toiling devoutly thus far, have shrunk back before that unexpected and appalling sign! Disciples of the living Lord, saints, philosophers, scholars, priests, knights, statesmen - what a throng! What thoughts there born, prayers there ended, vows there broken, light there breaking, hearts there torn in twain! Mighty mountain rock! rising full in the road of journeying humanity. Around its base the tides of the generations dividing as part the long racing billows of the sea about some awful cliff.

The lad closed his note-book, and taking his chair to the window, folded his arms on the sill and looked out. Soon he noticed what had escaped him before. Beyond the tree, at the foot of the ash-heap, a single dandelion had opened. It burned like a steadfast yellow lamp, low in the edge of the young grass. These two simple things - the locust leaves, touched by the sun, shaken by the south wind; the dandelion shining in the grass - awoke in him the whole vision of the spring now rising anew out of the Earth, all over the land: great Nature! And the vision of this caused him to think of something else.

On the Sunday following his talk with the lad, the pastor had preached the most arousing sermon that the lad had heard: it had grown out of that interview: it was on modern infidelity - the new infidelity as contrasted with the old.

In this sermon he had arraigned certain books as largely responsible. He called them by their titles. He warned his people against them. Here recommenced the old story: the lad was at once seized with a desire to read those books, thus exhibiting again the identical trait that had already caused him so much trouble. But this trait was perhaps himself - his core; the demand of his nature to hear both sides, to judge evidence, test things by his own reason, get at the deepest root of a matter: to see Truth, and to see Truth whole.

Curiously enough, these books, and some others, had been much heard of by the lad since coming to college: once; then several times; then apparently everywhere

James Lane Allen

and all the time. For, intellectually, they had become atmospheric: they had to be breathed, as a newly introduced vital element of the air, whether liked or not liked by the breathers. They were the early works of the great Darwin, together with some of that related illustrious group of scientific investigators and thinkers, who, emerging like promontories, islands, entire new countries, above the level of the world's knowledge, sent their waves of influence rushing away to every shore. It was in those years that they were flowing over the United States, over Kentucky. And as some volcanic upheaval under mid-ocean will in time rock the tiny boat of a sailor boy in some little sheltered bay on the other side of the planet, so the sublime disturbance in the thought of the civilized world in the second half of the nineteenth century had reached David.

Sitting at his window, looking out blindly for help and helpers amid his doubts, seeing the young green of the locust, the yellow of the dandelion, he recalled the names of those anathematized books, which were described as dealing so strangely with nature and with man's place in it. The idea dominated him at last to go immediately and get those books.

A little later he might have been seen quitting the dormitory and taking his way with a dubious step across the campus into the town.

Saturday forenoons of spring were busy times for the town in those days. Farmers were in, streets were crowded with their horses and buggies and rockaways, with live stock, with wagons hauling cord-wood, oats, hay, and hemp. Once, at a crossing, David waited while a wagon loaded with soft, creamy, gray hemp creaked past toward a factory. He sniffed with relish the tar of the mud-packed wheels; he put out a hand and stroked the heads drawn close in familiar bales.

Crowded, too, of Saturdays was the book-shop to which the students usually resorted for their supplies. Besides town customers and country customers, the pastor of the church often dropped in and sat near the stove, discoursing, perhaps, to some of his elders, or to reverent Bible students, or old acquaintances. A small, tight, hot, metal-smelling stove - why is it so enjoyable by a dogmatist?

As David made his way to the rear of the long bookshelves, which extended back toward the stove, the pastor rose and held out his hand with hearty warmth - and a glance of secret solicitude. The lad looked sheepish with embarrassment; not until accosted had he himself realized what a stray he had become from his pastor's flock and fold. And he felt that he ought instantly to tell the pastor this was the case. But the pastor had reseated himself and regripped his masterful monologue. The lad was more than embarrassed; he felt conscious of a new remorseful tenderness for this grim, righteous man, now that he had emancipated mind and conscience from his teaching: so true it often is that affection is possible only where obedience is not demanded. He turned off sorrowfully to the counter, and a few moments later, getting the attention of the clerk, asked in a low conscience-stricken tone for "The Origin of Species" and "The Descent of Man"; conscience-stricken at the sight of the money in his palm to pay for them.

"What are you going to do with these?" inquired a Bible student who had joined him at the counter and fingered the books.

"Read them," said the lad, joyously, "and understand them if I can."

He pinned them against his heart with his elbow and all but ran back to the dormitory. Having reached there, he altered his purpose and instead of mounting to his room, went away off to a quiet spot on the campus and, lying down in the grass under the wide open sky, opened his wide Darwin.

It was the first time in his life that he had ever encountered outside of the Bible a mind of the highest order, or listened to it, as it delivered over to mankind the astounding treasures of its knowledge and wisdom in accents of appealing, almost plaintive modesty.

That day the lad changed his teachers.

Of the session more than two months yet remained. Every few days he might have been seen at the store, examining books, drawing money reluctantly from his pocket, hurrying away with another volume. Sometimes he would deliver to the clerk the title of a work written on a slip of paper: an unheard-of book; to be ordered - perhaps from the Old World. For one great book inevitably leads to another. They have their parentage, kinship, generations. They are watch-towers in sight of each other on the same human highway. They are strands in a single cable belting the globe. Link by link David's investigating hands were slipping eagerly along a mighty chain of truths, forged separately by the giants of his time and now welded together in the glowing thought of the world.

Not all of these were scientific works. Some were works which followed in the wake of the new science, with rapid applications of its methods and results to other subjects, scarce conterminous or not even germane. For in the light of the great central idea of Evolution, all departments of human knowledge had to be reviewed, reconsidered, reconceived, rearranged, rewritten. Every foremost scholar of the world, kindling his own personal lamp at that central sunlike radiance, retired straightway into his laboratory of whatsoever kind and found it truly illuminated for the first time. His lamp seemed to be of two flames enwrapped as one; a baleful and a benign. Whenever it shone upon anything that was true, it made this stand out the more clear, valuable, resplendent. But wherever it uncovered the false, it darted thereat a swift tongue of flame, consuming without mercy the ancient rubbish of the mind. Vast purification of the world by the fire of truth! There have been such purifications before; but never perhaps in the history of the race was so much burned out of the intellectual path of man as during the latter half of the nineteenth century.

There is a sort of land which receives in autumn, year by year, the deposit of its own dead leaves and weeds and grasses without either the winds and waters to clear these away or the soil to reabsorb and reconvert them into the materials of reproduction. Thus year by year the land tends farther toward sterility by the very accumulation of what was once its life. But send a forest fire across those smothering strata of vegetable decay; give once more a chance for every root below to meet the sun above; for every seed above to reach the ground below; soon again the barren will be the fertile, the desert blossom as the rose. It is so with the human mind. It is ever putting forth a thousand things which are the expression of its life for a brief season. These myriads of things mature, ripen, bear their fruit, fall back dead upon the soil of the mind itself. That mind may be the mind of an individual; it may be the mind of a century, a race, a civilization. To the individual, then, to a race, a civilization, a century, arrives the hour when it must either consume its own dead or surrender its own life. These hours are the moral, the intellectual revolutions of history.

The new science must not only clear the stagnant ground for the growth of new ideas, it must go deeper. Not enough that rubbish should be burned: old structures of knowledge and faith, dangerous, tottering, unfit to be inhabited longer, must be shaken to their foundations. It brought on therefore a period of intellectual upheaval and of drift, such as was once passed through by the planet itself. What had long stood locked and immovable began to move; what had been high sank out of sight; what had been low was lifted. The mental hearing, listening as an ear placed amid still mountains, could gather into itself from afar the slip and fall of avalanches. Whole systems of belief which had chilled the soul for centuries, dropped off like icebergs into the warming sea and drifted away, melting into nothingness.

The minds of many men, witnessing this double ruin by flame and earthquake, are at such times filled with consternation: to them it seems that nothing will survive, that beyond these cataclysms there will never again be stability and peace - a new and better age, safer footing, wider horizons, clearer skies.

It was so now. The literature of the New Science was

followed by a literature of new Doubt and Despair. But both of these were followed by yet another literature which rejected alike the New Science and the New Doubt, and stood by all that was included under the old beliefs. The voices of these three literatures filled the world: they were the characteristic notes of that half-century, heard sounding together: the Old Faith, the New Science, the New Doubt. And they met at a single point; they met at man's place in Nature, at the idea of God, and in that system of thought and creed which is Christianity.

It was at this sublime meeting-place of the Great Three that this untrained and simple lad soon arrived - searching for the truth. Here he began to listen to them, one after another: reading a little in science (he was not prepared for that), a little in the old faith, but most in the new doubt. For this he was ready; toward this he had been driven.

Its earliest effects were soon exhibited in him as a student. He performed all required work, slighted no class, shirked no rule, transgressed no restriction. But he asked no questions of any man now, no longer roved distractedly among the sects, took no share in the discussions rife in his own church. There were changes more significant: he ceased to attend the Bible students' prayer-meeting at the college or the prayer-meeting of the congregation in the town; he would not say grace at those evening suppers of the Disciples; he declined the Lord's Supper; his voice was not heard in the choir. He was, singularly enough, in regular attendance at morning and night services of the church; but he entered timidly, apologetically, sat as near as possible to the door, and slipped out a little before the people were dismissed: his eyes had been fixed

James Lane Allen

respectfully on his pastor throughout the sermon, but his thoughts were in other temples.

VIII

The session reached its close. The students were scattered far among the villages, farms, cities of many states. Some never to return, having passed from the life of a school into the school of life; some, before vacation ended, gone with their laughter and vigor into the silence of the better Teacher.

Over at the dormitory the annual breaking-up of the little band of Bible students had, as always, been affecting. Calm, cool, bright day of June! when the entire poor tenement house was fragrant with flowers brought from commencement; when a south wind sent ripples over the campus grass; and outside the campus, across the street, the yards were glowing with roses. Oh, the roses of those young days, how sweet, how sweet they were! How much sweeter now after the long, cruel, evil suffering years which have passed and gone since they faded!

The students were dispersed, and David sat at his table by his open window, writing to his father and mother.

After telling them he had stood well in his classes, and giving some descriptions of the closing days and ceremonies of the college, for he knew how interested they would be in reading about these things, he announced that he was not coming home. He enclosed a part of the funds still on hand, and requested his father to hire a man in his place to work on the farm during the summer. He said nothing of his doubts and troubles, but gave as the reason of his remaining away what indeed the reason was: that he wished to study during the vacation; it was the best chance he had ever had, perhaps would ever have; and it was of the utmost importance to him to settle a great many questions before the next session of the Bible College opened. His expenses would be small. He had made arrangements with the wife of the janitor to take charge of his room and his washing and to give him his meals: his room itself would not cost him anything, and he did not need any more clothes.

It was hard to stay away from them. Not until separated, had he realized how dear they were to him. He could not bear even to write about all that. And he was homesick for the sight of the farm, - the horses and cows and sheep, - for the sight of Captain. But he must remain where he was; what he had to do must be done quickly - a great duty was involved. And they must write to him oftener because he would need their letters, their love, more than ever now. And so God keep them in health and bless them. And he was their grateful son, who too often had been a care to them, who could never forget the sacrifices they had made to send him to college, and whose only wish was that he might not cause them any disappointment in the future.

This letter drew a quick reply from his father. He returned the money, saying that he had done better on the farm than he had expected and did not need it, and that he had a man employed, his former slave. Sorry as they were not to see him that summer, still they were glad of his desire to study through vacation. His own life had not been very successful; he had tried hard, but had failed. For a longtime now he had been accepting the failure as best he could. But compensation for all this were the new interests, hopes, ambitions, which centred in the life of his son. To see him a minister, a religious leader among men - that would be happiness enough for him. His family had always been a religious people. One thing he was already looking forward to: he wanted his son to preach his first sermon in the neighborhood church founded by the lad's great-grandfather - that would be the proudest hour of his life and in the lad's mother's. There were times in the past when perhaps he had been hard on him, not understanding him; this only made his wish the greater to aid him now in every way, at any cost. When they were not talking of him at home, they were thinking of him. And they blessed God that He had given them such a son. Let him not be troubled about the future; they knew that he would never disappoint them.

David sat long immovable before that letter.

One other Bible student remained. On the campus, not far from the dormitory, stood a building of a single story, of several rooms. In one of these rooms there lived, with his family, that tall, gaunt, shaggy, middle-aged man, in his shiny black coat and paper collars, without any cravats, who had been the lad's gentle monitor on the morning of his entering college. He, too, was to spend the summer there, having no means of getting away with his wife and children. Though he sometimes went off himself, to hold meetings where he could and for what might be paid him; now preaching and baptizing in the mountains; now back again, laboring in his shirt-sleeves at the Pentateuch and the elementary structure of the English language. Such troubles as David's were not for him; nor science nor doubt. His own age contained him as a green field might hold a rock. Not that this kind, faithful, helpful soul was a lifeless stone; but that he was as unresponsive to the movements of his time as a boulder is to the energies of a field. Alive in his own sublime way he was, and inextricably rooted in one ever-living book alone - the Bible.

This middle-aged, childlike man, settled near David as his neighbor, was forever a reminder to him of the faith he once had had - the faith of his earliest youth, the faith of his father and mother. Sometimes when the day's work was done and the sober, still twilights came on, this reverent soul, sitting with his family gathered about him near the threshold of his single homeless room, - his oldest boy standing beside his chair, his wife holding in her lap the sleeping babe she had just nursed, - would begin to sing. The son's voice joined the father's; the wife's followed the son's, in their usual hymn: -

"How firm a foundation, ye saints of the Lord,
   Is laid for your faith in His excellent word."

Up in his room, a few hundred yards away, the lad that moment might be trimming his lamp for a little more reading. More than once he waited, listening in the darkness, to the reliant music of the stalwart, stern old poem. How devotedly he too had been used to sing it!

That summer through, then, he kept on at the work of trying to settle things before college reopened - things which involved a great duty. Where the new thought of the age attacked dogma, Revelation, Christianity most, there most he read. He was not the only reader. He was one of a multitude which no man could know or number; for many read in secret. Ministers of the Gospel read in secret in their libraries, and locked the books away when their church officers called unexpectedly. On Sunday, mounting their pulpits, they preached impassioned sermons concerning faith - addressed to the doubts, ravaging their own convictions and consciences.

Elders and deacons read and kept the matter hid from their pastors. Physicians and lawyers read and spoke not a word to their wives and children. In the church, from highest ecclesiastic and layman, wherever in the professions a religious, scientific, scholarly mind, there was felt the central intellectual commotion of those years - the Battle of the Great Three.

And now summer was gone, the students flocking in, the session beginning. David reentered his classes. Inwardly he drew back from this step; yet take any other, throw up the whole matter, - that he could not do. With all his lifelong religious sense he held on to the former realities, even while his grasp was loosening.

But this could not endure. University life as a Bible student and candidate for the ministry, every day and many times every day, required of him duties which he could not longer conscientiously discharge; they forced from him expressions regarding his faith which made it only too plain both to himself and to others how much out of place he now was.

So the crisis came, as come it must.

Autumn had given place to winter, to the first snows, thawing during the day, freezing at night. The roofs of the town were partly brown, partly white; icicles hung lengthening from the eaves. It was the date on which the university closed for the Christmas holidays - Friday afternoon preceding. All day through the college corridors, or along the snow-paths leading to the town, there had been the glad noises of that wild riotous time: whistle and song and shout and hurrying feet, gripping hands, good wishes, and good-bys. One by one the sounds had grown fewer, fainter, and had ceased; the college was left in emptiness and silence, except in a single lecture room in one corner of the building, from the windows of which you looked out across the town and toward the west; there the scene took place.

It was at the door of this room that the lad, having paused a moment outside to draw a deep, quivering breath, knocked, and being told to come in, entered, closed the door behind him, and sat down white and trembling in the nearest chair. About the middle of the room were seated the professors of the Bible College and his pastor. They rose, and calling him forward shook hands with him kindly, sorrowfully, and pointed to a seat before them, resuming their own.

Before them, then, sat the lad, facing the wintry light; and there was a long silence. Every one knew beforehand what the result would be. It was the best part of a year since that first interview in the pastor's study; there had been other interviews - with the pastor, with the professors. They had done what they could to check him, to bring him back. They had long been counsellors; now in duty they were authorities, sitting to hear him finally to the end, that they might pronounce sentence: that would be the severance of his connection with the university and his expulsion from the church.

Old, old scene in the history of Man - the trial of his Doubt by his Faith: strange day of judgment, when one half of the human spirit arraigns and condemns the other half. Only five persons sat in that room - four men and a boy. The room was of four bare walls and a blackboard, with perhaps a map or two of Palestine, Egypt, and the Roman Empire in the time of Paul. The era was the winter of the year 1868, the place was an old town of the Anglo-Saxon backwoodsmen, on the blue-grass highlands of Kentucky. But in how many other places has that scene been enacted, before what other audiences of the accusing and the accused, under what laws of trial, with what degrees and rigors of judgment! Behind David, sitting solitary there in the flesh, the imagination beheld a throng so countless as to have been summoned and controlled by the deep arraigning eye of Dante alone. Unawares, he stood at the head of an invisible host, which stretched backward through time till it could be traced no farther. Witnesses all to that sublime, indispensable part of man which is his Doubt - Doubt respecting his origin, his meaning, his Maker, and his destiny. That perpetual half-night of his planet-mind - that shadowed side of his orbit-life - forever attracted and held in place by the force of Deity, but destined never to receive its light. Yet from that chill, bleak side what things have not reached round and caught the sun! And as of the earth's plants, some grow best and are sweetest in darkness, what strange blossoms of faith open and are fragrant in that eternal umbra! Sacred, sacred Doubt of Man. His agony, his searching! which has led him always onward from more ignorance to less ignorance, from

James Lane Allen

less truth to more truth; which is the inspiration of his mind, the sorrow of his heart; which has spoken everywhere in his science, philosophy, literature, art - in his religion itself; which keeps him humble not vain, changing not immutable, charitable not bigoted; which attempts to solve the universe and knows that it does not solve it, but ever seeks to trace law, to clarify reason, and so to find whatever truth it can.

As David sat before his professors and his pastor, it was one of the moments that sum up civilization.

Across the room, behind them also, what a throng! Over on that side was Faith, that radiant part of the soul which directly basks in the light of God, the sun. There, visible to the eye of imagination, were those of all times, places, and races, who have sat in judgment on doubters, actual or suspected. In whatsoever else differing, united in this: that they have always held themselves to be divinely appointed agents of the Judge of all the earth: His creatures chosen to punish His creatures. And so behind those professors, away back in history, were ranged Catholic popes and Protestant archbishops, and kings and queens, Protestant and Catholic, and great mediaeval jurists, and mailed knights and palm-bearing soldiers of the cross, and holy inquisitors drowning poor old bewildered women, tearing living flesh from flesh as paper, crushing bones like glass, burning the shrieking human body to cinders: this in the name of a Christ whose Gospel was mercy, and by the authority of a God whose law was love. They were all there, tier after tier, row above row, a vast shadowy colosseum of intent judicial faces - Defenders of the Faith.

But no inquisitor was in this room now, nor punitive

intention, nor unkind thought. Slowly throughout the emerging life of man this identical trial has gained steadily in charity and mildness. Looking backward over his long pathway through bordering mysteries, man himself has been brought to see, time and again, that what was his doubt was his ignorance; what was his faith was his error; that things rejected have become believed, and that things believed have become rejected; that both his doubt and his faith are the temporary condition of his knowledge, which is ever growing; and that rend him faith and doubt ever will, but destroy him, never.

No Smithfield fire, then, no Jesuitical rack, no cup of hemlock, no thumb-screw, no torture of any kind for David. Still, here was a duty to be done, an awful responsibility to be discharged in sorrow and with prayer; and grave good men they were. Blameless was this lad in all their eyes save in his doubt. But to doubt - was not that the greatest of sins?

The lad soon grew composed. These judges were still his friends, not his masters. His masters were the writers of the books in which he believed, and he spoke for them, for what he believed to be the truth, so far as man had learned it. The conference lasted through that short winter afternoon. In all that he said the lad showed that he was full of many confusing voices: the voices of the new science, the voices of the new doubt. One voice only had fallen silent in him: the voice of the old faith.

It had grown late. Twilight was descending on the white campus, on the snow-capped town. Away in the west, beyond the clustered house-tops, there had formed itself the solemn picture of a red winter sunset.

James Lane Allen

The light entered the windows and fell on the lad's face. One last question had just been asked him by the most venerable and beloved of his professors - in tones awe-stricken, and tremulous with his own humility, and with compassion for the erring boy before him, -

"Do you not even believe in God?"

Ah, that question! which shuts the gates of consciousness upon us when we enter sleep, and sits close outside our eyelids as we waken; which was framed in us ere we were born, which comes fullest to life in us as life itself ebbs fastest. That question which exacts of the finite to affirm whether it apprehends the Infinite, that prodding of the evening midge for its opinion of the polar star.

"Do you not even believe in God?"

The lad stood up, he whose life until these months had been a prayer, whose very slumbers had been worship. He stood up, from some impulse - perhaps the respectful habit of rising when addressed in class by this professor. At first he made no reply, but remained looking over the still heads of his elders into that low red sunset sky. How often had he beheld it, when feeding the stock at frozen twilights. One vision rose before him now of his boyhood life at home - his hopes of the ministry - the hemp fields where he had toiled - his father and mother waiting before the embers this moment, mindful of him. He recalled how often, in the last year, he had sat upon his bedside at midnight when all were asleep, asking himself that question: -

"Do I believe in God?"

And now he was required to lay bare what his young soul had been able to do with that eternal mystery.

He thrust his big coarse hand into his breast-pocket and drew out a little red morocco Testament which had been given him when he was received into the congregation. He opened it at a place where it seemed used to lie apart. He held it before his face, but could not read. At last, controlling himself, he said to them with dignity, and with the common honesty which was the life of him: -

"I read you a line which is the best answer I can give just now to your last question."

And so he read: -

"Lord, I believe; help Thou my unbelief!"

A few moments later he turned to another page and said to them: -

"These lines also I desire to read to you who believe in Christ and believe that Christ and God are one. I may not understand them, but I have thought of them a great deal: - "

"'And if any man hear my words and believe not, I judge him not: for I came not to judge the world but to save the world.'"

"'He that rejecteth me and receiveth not my words, hath one that judgeth him: the word that I have spoken, the same shall judge him in the last day'"

He shut his Testament and put it back into his pocket

and looked at his judges.

"I understand this declaration of Christ to mean," he said, "that whether I believe in Him or do not believe in Him, I am not to be judged till God's Day of Judgment."

IX

A few days later David was walking across the fields on his way home: it was past the middle of the afternoon.

At early candle-light that morning, the huge red stage-coach, leaving town for his distant part of the country, had rolled, creaking and rattling, to the dormitory entrance, the same stage that had conveyed him thither. Throwing up his window he had looked out at the curling white breath of the horses and at the driver, who, buried in coats and rugs, and holding the lash of his whip in his mittened fist, peered up and called out with no uncertain temper.

The lad was ready. He hastily carried down the family umbrella and the Brussels carpet valise with its copious pink roses, looking strangely out of season amid all that hoar frost. Then he leaped back upstairs for something which had been added to his worldly goods since he entered college - a small, cheap trunk, containing a few garments and the priceless books. These things the driver stored in the boot of the stage, bespattered with mud now frozen. Then, running back once more, the lad seized his coat and hat, cast one troubled glance around the meaningless room which had been the theatre of such a drama in his life, went over to the little table, and blew out his Bible Student's lamp forever; and hurrying down with a cordial "all ready," climbed to the seat beside the driver and was whirled away.

He turned as he passed from the campus to take a last look at Morrison College, standing back there on the hill, venerable, majestical, tight-closed, its fires put out. As he crossed the city (for there were passengers to be picked up and the mail-bag to be gotten), he took unspoken leave of many other places: of the bookstore where he had bought the masterpieces of his masters; of the little Italian apple-man - who would never again have so simple a customer for his slightly damaged fruit; of several tall, proud, well-frosted church spires now turning rosy in the sunrise; of a big, handsome house standing in a fashionable street, with black coal smoke pouring out of the chimneys. There the friends of his boyhood "boarded"; there they were now, asleep in luxurious beds, or gone away for the holidays, he knew not which: all he did know was that they were gone far away from him along life's other pathways.

Soon the shops on each side were succeeded by homesteads; gradually these stood farther apart as farm-houses set back from the highroad; the street had become a turnpike, they were in open country and the lad was on his way to his father and mother.

In the afternoon, at one of the stops for watering horses, he had his traps and trappings put out. From this place a mud road wound across the country to his neighborhood; and at a point some two miles distant, a pair of bars tapped it as an outlet and inlet for the travel on his father's land.

Leaving his things at the roadside farmhouse with the

promise that he would return for them, the lad struck out - not by the lane, but straight across country.

It was a mild winter day without wind, without character - one of the days on which Nature seems to take no interest in herself and creates no interest in others. The sky was overcrowded with low, ragged clouds, without discernible order or direction. Nowhere a yellow sunbeam glinting on any object, but vast jets of misty radiance shot downward in far-diverging lines toward the world: as though above the clouds were piled the waters of light and this were scant escaping spray.

He walked on, climbing the fences, coming on the familiar sights of winter woods and fields. Having been away from them for the first time and that during more than a year, with what feelings he now beheld them!

Crows about the corn shocks, flying leisurely to the stake-and-ridered fence: there alighting with their tails pointing toward him and their heads turned sideways over one shoulder; but soon presenting their breasts seeing he did not hunt. The solitary caw of one of them - that thin, indifferent comment of their sentinel, perched on the silver-gray twig of a sycamore. In another field the startled flutter of field larks from pale-yellow bushes of ground-apple. Some boys out rabbit-hunting in the holidays, with red cheeks and gay woollen comforters around their hot necks and jeans jackets full of Spanish needles: one shouldering a gun, one carrying a game-bag, one eating an apple: a pack of dogs and no rabbit. The winter brooks, trickling through banks of frozen grass and broken reeds; their clear brown water sometimes open, sometimes covered with figured ice.

Red cattle in one distant wood, moving tender-footed around the edge of a pond. The fall of a forest tree sounding distinct amid the reigning stillness - felled for cord wood. And in one field - right there before him! - the chopping sound of busy hemp brakes and the sight of negroes, one singing a hymn. Oh, the memories, the memories!

By and by he reached the edge of his father's land, climbed to the topmost rail of the boundary fence and sat there, his eyes glued to the whole scene. It lay outspread before him, the entirety of that farm. He had never realized before how little there was of it, how little! He could see all around it, except where the woods hid the division fence on one side. And the house, standing in the still air of the winter afternoon, with its rotting roof and low red chimneys partly obscured by scraggy cedars - how small it had become! How poor, how wretched everything - the woodpile, the cabin, the hen-house, the ice-house, the barn! Was this any part of the great world? It was one picture of desolation, the creeping paralysis of a house and farm. Did anything even move?

Something did move. A column of blue smoke moved straight and thin from the chimney of his father's and mother's room. In a far corner of the stable lot, pawing and nozzling some remnants of fodder, were the old horses. By the hay-rick he discovered one of the sheep, the rest being on the farther side. The cows by and by filed slowly around from behind the barn and entered the doorless milking stalls. Suddenly his dog emerged from one of those stalls, trotting cautiously, then with a playful burst of speed went in a streak across the lot toward the kitchen. A negro man issued from the cabin, picked out a log, knocked the ashes out of his pipe in the palm of his hand, and began to cut the firewood for the night.

All this did not occur at once: he had been sitting there a long time - heart-sick with the thought of the tragedy he was bringing home. How could he ever meet them, ever tell them? How would they ever understand? If he could only say to his father: "I have sinned and I have broken your heart: but forgive me." But he could not say this: he did not believe that he had done wrong. Yet all that he would now have to show in their eyes would be the year of his wasted life, and a trunk full of the books that had ruined him.

Ah, those two years before he had started to college, during which they had lived happily together! Their pride in him! their self-denial, affection - all because he was to be a scholar and a minister!

He fancied he could see them as they sat in the house this moment, not dreaming he was anywhere near. One on each side of the fireplace; his mother wearing her black dress and purple shawl: a ball of yarn and perhaps a tea-cake in her lap; some knitting on her needles; she knit, she never mended. But his father would be mending - leather perhaps, and sewing, as he liked to sew, with hog bristles - the beeswax and the awls lying in the bottom of a chair drawn to his side. There would be no noises in the room otherwise: he could hear the stewing of the sap in the end of a fagot, the ticking of one clock, the fainter ticking of another in the adjoining room, like a disordered echo. They would not be talking; they would be thinking of him. He shut his eyes, compressed his lips, shook his head resolutely, and leaped down.

He had gone about twenty yards, when he heard a quick, incredulous bark down by the house and his dog appeared in full view, looking up that way, motionless. Then he came on running and barking resentfully, and a short distance off stopped again.

"Captain," he called with a quivering voice.

With ears laid back and one cry of joy the dog was on him. The lad stooped and drew him close. Neither at that moment had any articulate speech nor needed it. As soon as he was released, the dog, after several leaps toward his face, was off in despair either of expressing or of containing his joy, to tell the news at the house. David laggingly followed.

As he stepped upon the porch, piled against the wall beside the door were fagots as he used to see them. When he reached the door itself, he stopped, gazing foolishly at those fagots, at the little gray lichens on them: he could not knock, he could not turn the knob without knocking. But his step had been heard. His mother opened the door and peered curiously out.

"Why, it's Davy!" she cried. "Davy! Davy!"

She dropped her knitting and threw her arms around him.

"David! David!" exclaimed his father, with a glad proud voice inside. "Why, my son, my son!"

"Ah, he's sick - he's come home sick!" cried the mother, holding him a little way off to look at his face.

"Ah! the poor fellow's sick! Come in, come in. And this is why we had no letter! And to think yesterday was Christmas Day! And we had the pies and the turkey!"

"My son, are you unwell - have you been unwell? Sit here, lie here."

The lad's face was overspread with ghastly pallor; he had lost control of himself.

"I have not been sick. I am perfectly well," he said at length, looking from one to the other with forlorn, remorseful affection. They had drawn a chair close, one on each side of him. "How are you, mother? How are you, father?"

The change in HIM! - that was all they saw. As soon as he spoke, they knew he was in good health. Then the trouble was something else, more terrible. The mother took refuge in silence as a woman instinctively does at such times; the father sought relief in speech.

"What is the matter? What happened?"

After a moment of horrible silence, David spoke: -

"Ah, father! How can I ever tell you!"

"How can you ever tell me?"

The rising anger mingled with distrust and fear in those words! How many a father knows!

"Oh, what is it!" cried his mother, wringing her hands, and bursting into tears. She rose and went to her seat under the mantelpiece.

"What have you done?" said his father, also rising and going back to his seat.

There was a new sternness in his voice; but the look which returned suddenly to his eyes was the old life-long look.

The lad sat watching his father, dazed by the tragedy he was facing.

"It is my duty to tell you as soon as possible - I suppose I ought to tell you now."

"Then speak - why do you sit there - "

The words choked him.

"Oh! oh! - "

"Mother, don't! - "

"What is it?"

"Father, I have been put out of college and expelled from the church."

How loud sounded the minute noises of the fire - the clocks - the blows of an axe at the woodpile - the lowing of a cow at the barn.

"FOR WHAT?"

The question was put at length in a voice flat and dead. It summed up a lifetime of failure and admitted it.

After an interval it was put again: -

"FOR WHAT?"

"I do not believe the Bible any longer. I do not believe in Christianity."

"Oh, don't do THAT!"

The cry proceeded from David's mother, who crossed quickly and sat beside her husband, holding his hand, perhaps not knowing her own motive.

This, then, was the end of hope and pride, the reward of years of self-denial, the insult to all this poverty. For the time, even the awful nature of his avowal made no impression.

After a long silence, the father asked feebly: -

"WHY HAVE YOU COME BACK HERE?"

Suddenly he rose, and striding across to his son, struck him one blow with his mind: -

"OH, I ALWAYS KNEW THERE WAS NOTHING IN YOU!"

It was a kick of the foot.

X

More than two months had passed. Twilight of closing February was falling over the frozen fields. The last crow had flapped low and straight toward the black wood beyond the southern horizon. No sunset radiance streamed across the wide land, for all day a solitude of cloud had stretched around the earth, bringing on the darkness now before its time.

In a small hemp field on an edge of the vast Kentucky table-land, a solitary breaker kept on at his work. The splintered shards were piled high against his brake: he had not paused to clear them out of his way except around his bootlegs. Near by, the remnant of the shock had fallen over, clods of mingled frost and soil still sticking to the level butt-ends. Several yards to windward, where the dust and refuse might not settle on it, lay the pile of gray-tailed hemp, - the coarsest of man's work, but finished as conscientiously as an art. From the warming depths of this, rose the head and neck of a common shepherd dog, his face turned uneasily but patiently toward the worker. Whatever that master should do, whether understood or not, was right to him; he did not ask to understand, but to love and to serve. Farther away in another direction leaned the charred rind of a rotting stump. At intervals the rising wind blew the ashes away, exposing live coals - that fireside of the laborer, wandering with him from spot to spot over the bitter lonely spaces.

The hemp breaker had just gone to the shock and torn away another armful, dragging the rest down. Exhausting to the picked and powerful, the work seemed easy to him; for he was a young man of the greatest size and strength, moulded in the proportions which Nature often chooses for her children of the soil among that people. Striding rapidly back to his brake, the clumsy five-slatted device of the pioneer Kentuckians, he raised the handle and threw the armful of stalks crosswise between the upper and the lower blades. Then swinging the handle high, with his body wrenched violently forward and the strength of his good right arm put forth, he brought it down. The CRASH, CRASH, CRASH could have been heard far through the still air; for it is the office of those dull blades to hack their way as through a bundle of dead rods.

A little later he stopped abruptly, with silent inquiry turning his face to the sky: a raindrop had fallen on his hand. Two or three drops struck his face as he waited. It had been very cold that morning, too cold for him to come out to work. Though by noon it had moderated, it was cold still; but out of the warmer currents of the upper atmosphere, which was now the noiseless theatre of great changes going forward unshared as yet by the strata below, sank these icy globules of the winter rain. Their usual law is to freeze during descent into the crystals of snow; rarely they harden after they fall, covering the earth with sleet.

David, by a few quick circular motions of the wrist, freed his left hand from the half-broken hemp, leaving the bundle trailing across the brake. Then he hurried to the heap of well-cleaned fibre: that must not be allowed to get wet. The dog leaped out and stood to one side, welcoming the end of the afternoon labor and the idea of returning home. Not many minutes were required for the hasty baling, and David soon rested a moment beside his hemp, ready to lift it to his shoulders. But he felt disappointed. There lay the remnant of the shock. He had worked hard to finish it before sunset Would there not still be time?

The field occupied one of the swelling knolls of the landscape; his brake was set this day on the very crown of a hill. As he asked himself that question, he lifted his eyes and far away through the twilight, lower down, he saw the flash of a candle already being carried about in the kitchen. At the opposite end of the house the glow of firelight fell on the window panes of his father's and mother's room. Even while he observed this, it was intercepted: his mother thus early was closing the shutters for the night.

Too late! He gave up the thought of finishing his shock, recollecting other duties. But he remained in his attitude a few moments; for the workman has a curious unconscious habit of taking a final survey of the scene of his labor before quitting it. David now glanced first up at the sky, with dubious forethought of to-morrow's weather. The raindrops had ceased to fall, but he was too good a countryman not to foresee unsettled conditions. The dog standing before him and watching his face, uttered an uneasy whine as he noted that question addressed to the clouds: at intervals during the afternoon he had been asking his question also. Then those live coals in the rind of the stump and the danger of sparks blown to the hemp herds or brake, or fence farther away: David walked over and stamped them out. As he returned, he fondled the dog's head in his big, roughened hand.

"Captain," he said, "are you hungry?"

All at once he was attracted by a spectacle and forgot everything else. For as he stood there beside his bale of hemp in the dead fields, his throat and eyes filled with dust, the dust all over him, low on the dark red horizon there had formed itself the solemn picture of a winter sunset. Amid the gathering darkness the workman remained gazing toward that great light - into the stillness of it - the loneliness - the eternal peace. On his rugged face an answering light was kindled, the glory of a spiritual passion, the flame of immortal things alive in his soul. More akin to him seemed that beacon fire of the sky - more nearly his real pathway home appeared that distant road and gateway to the Infinite - than the flickering, near house-taper in the valley below. Once before, on the most memorable day of his life, David had beheld a winter sunset like that; but then across the roofs of a town - roofs half white, half brown with melting snow, and with lengthening icicles dripping in the twilight.

Suddenly, as if to shut out troubled thoughts, he stooped and, throwing his big, long arms about the hemp, lifted it to his shoulder. "Come, Captain," he called to his companion, and stalked heavily away. As he went, he began to hum an ancient, sturdy hymn: -

> "How firm a foundation, ye saints of the Lord,
> Is laid for your faith in His excellent Word.
> The flame shall not hurt thee; I only design
> Thy dross to consume and thy gold to refine."

He had once been used to love those words and to feel the rocklike basis of them as fixed unshakably beneath the rolling sea of the music; now he sang the melody only. A little later, as though he had no right to indulge himself even in this, it died on the air; and only the noise of his thick, stiffened boots could have been heard crushing the frozen stubble, as he went staggering under his load toward the barn.

XI

When he reached the worm fence of the hemp field, he threw his load from his shoulder upon the topmost rail, and, holding it there with one hand, climbed over. He had now to cross the stable lot. Midway of this, he passed a rick of hay. Huddled under the sheltered side were the sheep of the farm, several in number and of the common sort. At the sight of him, they always bleated familiarly, but this evening their long, quavering, gray notes were more penetrating, more insistent than usual. These sensitive, gentle creatures, whose instincts represent the accumulating and inherited experiences of age upon age of direct contact with nature, run far ahead of us in our forecasting wisdom; and many a time they utter their disquietude and warning in language that is understood only by themselves. The scant flock now fell into the wake of David, their voices blending in a chorus of meek elegiacs, their fore feet crowding close upon his heels. The dog, yielding his place, fell into their wake, as though covering the rear; and so this little procession of friends moved in a close body toward the barn.

David put his hemp in the saddle-house; a separate hemp-house they were not rich enough to own. He had chosen this particular part of the barn because it was dryest in roof and floor. Several bales of hemp were already piled against the logs on one side; and besides these, the room contained the harness, the cart and the wagon gear, the box of tar, his maul and wedges, his saddle and bridle, and sundry implements used in the garden or on the farm. It was almost dark in there now, and he groped his way.

The small estate of his father, comprising only some fifty or sixty acres, supported little live stock: the sheep just mentioned, a few horses, several head of cattle, a sow and pigs. Every soul of these inside or outside the barn that evening had been waiting for David. They had begun to think of him and call for him long before he had quit work in the field. Now, although it was not much later than usual, the heavy cloud made it appear so; and all these creatures, like ourselves, are deceived by appearances and suffer greatly from imagination. They now believed that it was far past the customary time for him to appear, that they were nearing the verge of starvation; and so they were bewailing in a dejected way his unaccountable absence and their miserable lot - with no one to listen.

Scarcely had the rattling of the iron latch of the saddle-house apprised them of his arrival before every dumb brute - dumb, as dumb men say - experienced a cheerful change of mind, and began to pour into his ears the eager, earnest, gratifying tale of its rights and its wrongs. What honest voices as compared with the human - sometimes. No question of sincerity could have been raised by any one who heard THEM speak. It may not have been music; but every note of it was God's truth.

The man laughed heartily as he paused a moment and listened to that rejoicing uproar. But he was touched, also. To them he was the answerer of prayer. Not one believed that he ever refused to succor in time of need, or turned a deaf ear to supplication. If he made poor provision for them sometimes, though they might not feel satisfied, they never turned against him. The barn was very old. The chemical action of the elements had first rotted away the shingles at the points where the nails pinned them to the roof; and, thus loosened, the winds of many years had dislodged and scattered them. Through these holes, rain could penetrate to the stalls of the horses, so that often they would get up mired and stiff and shivering; but they never reproached him. On the northern side of the barn the weather-boarding was quite gone in places, and the wind blew freely in. Of winter mornings the backs of the cows would sometimes be flecked with snow, or this being stubbornly melted by their own heat, their hides would be hung with dew-drops: they never attributed that fact to him as a cruelty. In the whole stable there was not one critic of his providence: all were of the household of faith: the members being in good standing and full fellowship.

Remembrance of this lay much in his mind whenever, as often, he contrasted his association with his poor animals, and the troublous problem of faith in his own soul. It weighed with especial heaviness upon his heart, this nightfall in the barn, over which hung that threatening sky. Do what he could for their comfort, it must be insufficient in a rotting, windswept shelter like that. And here came the pinch of conscience, the wrench of remorse: the small sums of money which his father and mother had saved up at such a sacrifice on the farm, - the money which he had spent lavishly on himself in preparation, as he had supposed, for his high calling in life, - if but a small part of that had been applied to the roof and weather-boarding of the stable, the stock this night might have been housed in warmth and safety.

The feeding and bedding attended to, with a basket of cobs in his hand for his mother, he hurried away to the woodpile. This was in the yard near the negro cabin and a hundred yards or more from the house. There he began to cut and split the wood for the fires that night and for next morning. Three lengths of this: first, for the grate in his father's and mother's room - the best to be found among the logs of the woodpile: good dry hickory for its ready blaze and rousing heat; to be mixed with seasoned oak, lest it burn out too quickly - an expensive wood; and perhaps also with some white ash from a tree he had felled in the autumn. Then sundry back-logs and knots of black walnut for the cabin of the two negro women (there being no sense of the value of this wood in the land in those days, nearly all of it going to the cabins, to the kitchens, to cord-wood, or to the fences of the farm; while the stumps were often grubbed up and burned on the spot). Then fuel of this same sort for the kitchen stove. Next, two or three big armfuls of very short sticks for the small grate in his own small room above stairs - a little more than usual, with the idea that he might wish to sit up late.

There was scarce light enough to go by. He picked his logs from the general pile by the feel of the bark; and having set his foot on each, to hold it in place while he chopped, he struck rather by habit than by sight. Loud and rapid the strokes resounded; for he went at it with a youthful will, and with hunger gnawing him; and though his arms were stiff and tired, the axe to him was always a plaything - a plaything that he loved. At last, from under the henhouse near by he drew out and split some pieces of kindling, and then stored his axe in that dry place with fresh concern about soft weather: for more raindrops were falling and the wind was rising.

Stooping down now, he piled the fagots in the hollow of his arm, till the wood rose cold and damp against his hot neck, against his ear, and carried first some to the kitchen; and then some to the side porch of the house, where he arranged it carefully against the wall, close to the door, and conveniently for a hand reaching outward from within. As he was heaping up the last of it, having taken three turns to the woodpile, the door was opened slowly, and a slight, slender woman peered around at him.

"What makes you so late?"

Her tone betrayed minute curiosity rather than any large concern.

"I wanted to finish a shock, mother. But it isn't much later than usual; it's the clouds. Here's some good kindling for you in the morning and a basket of cobs," he added tenderly.

She received in silence the feed basket he held out to her, and watched him as he kneeled, busily piling up the last of the fagots.

"I hope you haven't cut any more of that green oak; your father couldn't keep warm."

"This is hickory, dead hickory, with some seasoned oak. Father'll have to take his coat off and you'll have to get a fan."

There was a moment of silence.

"Supper's over," she said simply.

She held in one hand a partly eaten biscuit.

"I'll be in soon now. I've nothing to do but kindle my fire."

After another short interval she asked:

"Is it going, to snow?"

"It's going to do something."

She stepped slowly back into the warm room and closed the door.

David hurried to the woodpile and carried the sticks for his own grate upstairs, making two trips of it. The stairway was dark; his room dark and damp, and filled with the smell of farm boots and working clothes left wet in the closets. Groping his way to the mantelpiece, he struck a sulphur match, lighted a half-burned candle, and kneeling down, began to kindle his fire.

As it started and spread, little by little it brought out of the cheerless darkness all the features of the rough, homely, kind face, bent over and watching it so impatiently and yet half absently. It gave definition to the shapeless black hat, around the brim of which still hung filaments of tow, in the folds of which lay white splinters of hemp stalk. There was the dust of field and barn on the edges of the thick hair about the ears; dust around the eyes and the nostrils. He was resting on one knee; over the other his hands were crossed - enormous, powerful, coarsened hands, the skin so frayed and chapped that around the finger-nails and along the cracks here and there a little blood had oozed out and dried.

James Lane Allen

XII

When David came down to his supper, all traces of the day's labor that were removable had disappeared. He was clean; and his working clothes had been laid aside for the cheap black-cloth suit, which he had been used to wear on Sundays while he was a student. Grave, gentle, looking tired but looking happy, with his big shock head of hair and a face rugged and majestical like a youthful Beethoven. A kind mouth, most of all, and an eye of wonderfully deep intelligence.

The narrow, uncarpeted stairway down which he had noisily twisted his enormous figure, with some amusement, as always, had brought him to the dining room. This was situated between the kitchen and his father's and mother's bedroom. The door of each of these stood ajar, and some of the warmth of the stove on one side and of the grate on the other dried and tempered the atmosphere.

His mother sat in her place at the head of the table, quietly waiting for him, and still holding in one hand the partially eaten biscuit As he took his seat, she rose, and, walking listlessly to the kitchen door, made a listless request of one of the two negro women. When the coffee had been brought in, standing, she poured out a cup, sweetened, stirred, and tasted it, and putting the spoon into it, placed it before him. Then she resumed her seat (and the biscuit) and looked on, occasionally scrutinizing his face, with an expression perhaps the most tragic that can ever be worn by maternal eyes: the expression of a lowly mother who has given birth to a lofty son, and who has neither the power to understand him, nor the grace to realize her own inferiority.

She wore, as usual, a dress of plain mourning, although she had not the slightest occasion to mourn - at least, from the matter of death. In the throat of this was caught a large, thin, oval-shaped breastpin, containing a plait of her own and her husband's hair, braided together; and through these there ran a silky strand cut from David's head when an infant, and long before the parents discovered how unlike their child was to themselves. This breastpin, with the hair of the three heads of the house intertwined, was the only symbol in all the world of their harmony or union.

Around her shoulders she had thrown, according to her wont, a home-knit crewel shawl of black and purple. Her hair, thick and straight and pasted down over the temples of her small head, looked like a long-used wig. Her contracted face seemed to have accumulated the wrinkles of the most drawn-out, careworn life. Yet she was not old; and these were not the lines of care; for her years had been singularly uneventful and - for her - happy. The markings were, perhaps, inherited from the generations of her weather-beaten, toiling, plain ancestors - with the added creases of her own personal habits. For she lived in her house with the regularity and contentment of an insect in a dead log. And few causes age the body faster than such wilful indolence and monotony of mind as hers - the mind, that very principle of physical youthfulness. Save only that it can also kill the body ere it age it; either by too great rankness breaking down at once the framework on which it has been reared, or afterward causing this to give way slowly under the fruitage of thoughts, too heavy any longer to be borne.

That from so dark a receptacle as this mother there should have emerged such a child of light, was one of those mysteries that are the perpetual delight of Nature and the despair of Science. This did not seem one of those instances - also a secret of the great Creatress - in which she produces upon the stem of a common rose a bud of alien splendor. It was as if potter's clay had conceived marble. The explanation of David did not lie in the fact that such a mother had produced him.

One of the truest marks of her small, cold mind was the rigid tyranny exercised over it by its own worthless ideas. Had she not sat beside her son while he ate, had she not denied herself the comfort of the fireside in the adjoining room, in order that she might pour out for him the coffee that was unfit to be drunk, she would have charged herself with being an unfaithful, undutiful mother. But this done, she saw no further, beheld nothing of the neglect, the carelessness, the cruelty, of all the rest, part of which this very moment was outspread beneath her eyes.

For at the foot of the table, where David's father had sat, were two partly eaten dishes: one of spare-rib, one of sausage. The gravy in each had begun to whiten into lard. Plates heaped with cornbread and with biscuit, poorly baked and now cold, were placed on each side. In front of him had been set a pitcher of milk; this rattled, as he poured it, with its own bluish ice. On all that homely, neglected board one thing only put everything else to shame. A single candle, in a low, brass candlestick in the middle of the table, scarce threw enough light to reveal the scene; but its flame shot deep into the golden, crystalline depths of a jar of honey standing close beside it - honey from the bees in the garden - a scathing but unnoticed rebuke from the food and housekeeping of the bee to the food and housekeeping of the woman.

Work in the hemp fields leaves a man's body calling in every tissue for restoration of its waste. David had hardly taken his seat before his eye swept the prospect before him with savage hope. In him was the hunger, not of toil alone, but of youth still growing to manhood, of absolute health. Whether he felt any mortification at his mother's indifference is doubtful. Assuredly life-long experience had taught him that nothing better was to be expected from her. How far he had unconsciously grown callous to things as they were at home, there is no telling. Ordinarily we become in such matters what we must; but it is likewise true that the first and last proof of high personal superiority is the native, irrepressible power of the mind to create standards which rise above all experience and surroundings; to carry everywhere with itself, whether it will or not, a blazing, scorching censorship of the facts that offend it. Regarding the household management of his mother, David at least never murmured; what he secretly felt he alone knew, perhaps not even he, since he was no self-examiner. As to those shortcomings of hers which he could not fail to see, for them he unconsciously showed tenderest compassion.

She had indulged so long her sloth even in the operation of thinking, that few ideas now rose from the

James Lane Allen

inner void to disturb the apathetic surface; and she did not hesitate to recur to any one of these any number of times in a conversation with the same person.

"What makes you so late?"

"I wanted to finish a shock. Then there was the feeding, and the wood to cut. And I had to warm my room up a little before I could wash."

"Is it going to snow?"

"It's hard to say. The weather looks very unsettled and threatening. That's one reason why I wanted to finish my shock."

There was silence for a while. David was too ravenous to talk; and his mother's habit was to utter one sentence at a time.

"I got three fresh eggs to-day; one had dropped from the roost and frozen; it was cracked, but it will do for the coffee in the morning."

"Winter must be nearly over if the hens are beginning to lay: THEY know. They must have some fresh nests."

"The cook wants to kill one of the old ones for soup to-morrow."

"What an evil-minded cook!"

It was with his mother only that David showed the new cheerfulness that had begun to manifest itself in him since his return from college. She, however, did not understand the reasons of this and viewed it unfavorably.

"We opened a hole in the last hill of turnips to-day."

She spoke with uneasiness.

"There'll be enough to last, I reckon, mother."

"You needn't pack any more chips to the smoke-house: the last meat's smoked enough."

"Very well, then. You shall have every basketful of them for your own fire."

"If you can keep them from the negroes: negroes love chips."

"I'll save them while I chop. You shall have them, if I have to catch them as they fly."

His hunger had been satisfied: his spirits began to rise.

"Mother, are you going to eat that piece of biscuit? If not, just hand it over to me, please."

She looked dryly down at the bread in her fingers: humor was denied her - that playfulness of purest reason.

David had commenced to collect a plateful of scraps - the most appetizing of the morsels that he himself had not devoured. He rose and went out into the porch to the dog.

" Now, mother , " he said, reentering; and with quiet

dignity he preceded her into the room adjoining.

His father sat on one side of the fireplace, watching the open door for the entrance of his son. He appeared slightly bent over in his chair. Plainly the days of rough farm-work and exposure were over for him, prematurely aged and housed. There was about him - about the shape and carriage of the head - in the expression of the eye most of all, perhaps, - the not wholly obliterated markings of a thoughtful and powerful breed of men. His appearance suggested that some explanation of David might be traceable in this quarter. For while we know nothing of these deep things, nor ever shall, in the sense that we can supply the proofs of what we conjecture; while Nature goes ever about her ancient work, and we cannot declare that we have ever watched the operations of her fingers, think on we will, and reason we must, amid her otherwise intolerable mysteries. Though we accomplish no more in our philosophy than the poor insect, which momentarily illumines its wandering through the illimitable night by a flash from its own body.

Lost in obscurity, then, as was David's relation to his mother, there seemed some gleams of light discernible in that between father and son. For there are men whom nature seems to make use of to connect their own offspring not with themselves but with earlier sires. They are like sluggish canals running between far-separated oceans - from the deeps of life to the deeps of life, allowing the freighted ships to pass. And no more does the stream understand what moves across its surface than do such commonplace agents comprehend the sons who have sprung from their own loins. Here, too, is one of Nature's greatest cruelties to the parent.

As David's father would not have recognized his remote ancestors if brought face to face, so he did not discover in David the image of them - the reappearance in the world, under different conditions, of certain elements of character found of old in the stock and line. He could not have understood how it was possible for him to transmit to the boy a nature which he himself did not actively possess. And, therefore, instead of beholding here one of Nature's mysterious returns, after a long period of quiescence, to her suspended activities and the perpetuation of an interrupted type, so that his son was but another strong link of descent joined to himself, a weak one; instead of this, he saw only with constant secret resentment that David was at once unlike him and his superior.

These two had worked side by side year after year on the farm; such comradeship in labor usually brings into consciousness again the primeval bond of Man against Nature - the brotherhood, at least, of the merely human. But while they had mingled their toil, sweat, hopes, and disappointments, their minds had never met. The father had never felt at home with his son; David, without knowing why - and many a sorrowful hour it had cost him - had never accepted as father the man who had brought him into the world. Each soon perceived that a distance separated them which neither could cross, though vainly both should try, and often both did try, to cross it.

As he sat in the chimney-corner to-night, his very look as he watched the door made it clear that he dreaded the entrance of his son; and to this feeling had lately been added deeper estrangement.

When David walked in, he took a seat in front of the fire. His mother followed, bringing the sugar-bowl and the honey, which she locked in a closet in the wall: the iron in her blood was parsimony. Then she seated herself under the mantelpiece on the opposite side and looked silently across at the face of her husband. (She was his second wife. His offspring by his first wife had died young. David was the only child of mature parents.) She looked across at him with the complacent expression of the wife who feels that she and her husband are one, even though their offspring may not be of them. The father looked at David; David looked into the fire. There was embarrassment all round.

"How are you feeling to-night, father?" he asked affectionately, a moment later, without lifting his eyes.

"I've been suffering a good deal. I think it's the weather."

"I'm sorry."

"Do you think it's going to snow?"

The husband had lived so long and closely with his wife, that the mechanism of their minds moved much like the two wall-clocks in adjoining rooms of the house; which ticked and struck, year after year, never quite together and never far apart. When David was first with one and then with another, he was often obliged to answer the same questions twice - some-times thrice, since his mother alone required two identical responses. He replied now with his invariable and patient courtesy - yet scarcely patient, inasmuch as this did not try him.

"What made you so late?"

David explained again.

"How much hemp did you break?"

"I didn't weigh it, father. Fifty or sixty pounds, perhaps."

"How many more shocks are there in the field?"

"Twelve or fifteen. I wish there were a hundred."

"I wish so, too," said David's mother, smiling plaintively at her husband.

"John Bailey was here after dinner," remarked David's father. "He has sold his crop of twenty-seven acres for four thousand dollars. Ten dollars a hundred."

"That's fine," said David with enthusiasm, thinking regretfully of their two or three acres.

"Good hemp lands are going to rent for twenty or twenty-five dollars an acre in the spring," continued his father, watching the effect of his words.

David got up, and going to the door, reached around against the wall for two or three sticks of the wood he had piled there. He replenished the fire, which was going down, and resumed his seat.

For a while father and son discussed in a reserved way matters pertaining to the farm: the amount of feed in the barn and the chances of its lasting; crops to be sown in the spring, and in what fields; the help they should hire - a new trouble at that time. For the negroes, recently emancipated, were wandering hither and thither over the farms, or flocking to the towns, unused to freedom, unused to the very wages they now demanded, and nearly everywhere seeking employment from any one in preference to their former masters as part of the proof that they were no longer in slavery. David's father had owned but a single small family of slaves: the women remained, the man had sought work on one of the far richer estates in the neighborhood.

They threshed over once more the straw of these familiar topics and then fell into embarrassed silence. The father broke this with an abrupt, energetic exclamation and a sharp glance: -

"If hemp keeps up to what it is now, I am going to put in more."

"Where?" asked the son, quietly. "I don't see that we have any ground to spare."

"I'll take the woods."

"FATHER!" cried David, wheeling on him.

"I'll take the woods!" repeated his father, with a flash of anger, of bitterness. "And if I'm not able to hire the hands to clear it, then I'll rent it. Bailey wants it. He offered twenty-five dollars an acre. Or I'll sell it," he continued with more anger, more bitterness. "He'd rather buy it than rent."

"How could we do without the woods?" inquired the son, looking like one dazed, - "without the timber and the grazing?"

"What will we do without the woods?" cried his father, catching up the words excitedly. "What will we do without the FARM?"

"What do you mean by all this, father? What is back of it?" cried David, suddenly aroused by vague fears.

"I mean," exclaimed the father, with a species of satisfaction in his now plain words, "I mean that Bailey wants to buy the farm. I mean that he urges me to sell out for my own good! tells me I must sell out! must move! leave Kentucky! go to Missouri - like other men when they fail."

"Go to Missouri," echoed the wife with dismal resignation, smiling at her husband.

"Have you sold it?" asked David, with flushed, angry face.

"No."

"Nor promised?"

"No!"

"Then, father, don't! Bailey is trying again to get the farm away from you. You and mother shall never sell your home and move to Missouri on my account."

The son sat looking into the fire, controlling his feelings. The father sat looking at the son, making a greater effort to control his. Both of them realized the poverty of the place and the need of money.

The hour was already past the father's early bed-time. He straightened himself up now, and turning his back, took off his coat, hung it on the back of his chair, and began to unbutton his waistcoat, and rub his arms. The mother rose, and going to the high-posted bed in a corner of the room, arranged the pillows, turned down the covers, and returning, sat provisionally on the edge of her chair and released her breastpin. David started up.

"Mother, give me a candle, will you?"

He went over with her to the closet, waited while she unlocked it and, thrusting her arm deep into its disordered depths, searched till she drew out a candle. No good-night was spoken; and David, with a look at his father and mother which neither of them saw, opened and closed the door of their warm room, and found himself in the darkness outside at the foot of the cold staircase.

XIII

A bed of crimson coals in the bottom of the grate was all that survived of his own fire.

He sat down before it, not seeing it, his candle unlighted in his hand, a tragedy in his eyes.

A comfortless room. Rag carpeting on the floor. No rug softening the hearth-stones. The sashes of the windows loose in the frames and shaken to-night by twisty gusts. A pane of glass in one had been broken and the opening pasted over with a sheet of letter paper. This had been burst by an indolent hand, thrust through to close the shutters outside; and a current of cold air now swept across the small room. The man felt it, shook himself free of depressing thoughts, rose resolutely. He took from a closet one of his most worthless coats, and rolling it into a wad, stopped the hole. Going back to the grate, he piled on the wood, watching the blaze as it rushed up over the logs, devouring the dried lichens on the bark; then sinking back to the bottom rounds, where it must slowly rise again, reducing the wood to ashes. Beside him as he sat in his rush-bottomed chair stood a small square table and on this a low brass candlestick, the companion of the one in the dining room. A half-burnt candle rose out of the socket. As David now lighted it and laid the long fresh candle alongside the snuffers, he measured with his eye the length of his luminaries and the amount of his wood - two friends. The little grate had commenced to roar at him bravely, affectionately; and the candle sputtered to him and threw sparks into the air - the rockets of its welcoming flame.

It was not yet ten o'clock: two hours of the long winter evening remained. He turned to his treasury.

This was a trunk in a corner, the trunk he had bought while at college, small and cheap in itself, not in what it held. For here were David's books - the great grave books which had been the making of him, or the undoing of him, according as one may have enough of God's wisdom and mercy to decide whether it were the one or the other.

As the man now moved his chair over, lifted the lid, and sat gazing down at the backs of them, arranged in a beautiful order of his own, there was in the lofty, solemn look of him some further evidence of their power over him. The coarse toil of the day was forgotten; his loved dependent animals in the wind-swept barn forgotten; the evening with his father and mother, the unalterable emptiness of it, the unkindness, the threatening tragedy, forgotten. Not that desolate room with firelight and candle; not the poor farmhouse; not the meagre farm, nor the whole broad Kentucky plateau of fields and woods, heavy with winter wealth, heavy with comfortable homesteads - any longer held him as domicile, or native region: he was gone far away into the company of his high-minded masters, the writers of those books. Choosing one, he closed the lid of the trunk reluctantly over the rest, and with the book in one hand and the chair in the other, went back to the fire.

An hour passed, during which, one elbow on the table, the shaded side of his face supported in the palm of his hand, he read, scarce moving except to snuff the wick or to lay on a fresh fagot. At the end of this time other laws than those which the writer was tracing began to assert their supremacy over David - the laws of strength and health, warmth and weariness. Sleep was descending on him, relaxing his limbs, spreading a quiet mist through his brain, caressing his eyelids. He closed the pages and turned to his dying fire. The book caused him to wrestle; he wanted rest.

And now, floating to him through that mist in his brain, as softly as a nearing melody, as radiantly as dawning light, came the image of Gabriella: after David had pursued Knowledge awhile he was ready for Love. But knowledge, truth, wisdom before every other earthly passion - that was the very soul of him. His heart yearned for her now in this closing hour, when everything else out of his way, field-work, stable-work, wood-cutting, filial duties, study, he was alone with the thought of her, the newest influence in his life, taking heed of her solely, hearkening only to his heart's need of her. In all his rude existence she was the only being he had ever known who seemed to him worthy of a place in the company of his great books. Had the summons come to pack his effects to-morrow and, saying good-by to everything else, start on a journey to the congenial places where his mighty masters lived and wrought, he would have wished her alone to go with him, sharer of life's loftiness. Her companionship wherever he might be - to have just that; to feel that she was always with him, and always one with him; to be able to turn his eyes to hers before some vanishing firelight at an hour like this, with deep rest near them side by side!

He lingered over the first time he had ever seen her; that memorable twilight in the town, the roofs and chimneys of the houses, half-white, half-brown with melting snow, outlined against the low red sunset sky. He had not long before left the room in the university where his trial had taken place, and where he had learned that it was all over with him. He was passing along one of the narrow cross streets, when at a certain point his course was barred by a heap of fresh cedar boughs, just thrown out of a wagon. Some children were gay and busy, carrying them through the side doors, the sexton aiding. Other children inside the lighted church were practising a carol to organ music; the choir of their voices swelled out through the open doors, and some of the little ones, tugging at the cedar, took up the strain.

She was standing on the low steps of the church, in charge of the children. In one hand she held an unfinished wreath, and she was binding the dark, shining leaves with the other. A swarm of snowflakes, scarce more than glittering crystals, danced merrily about her head and flecked her black fur on one shoulder. As David, not very mindful just then of whither he was going, stepped forward across the light and paused before the pile of cedar boughs, she glanced at him with a smile, seeing how his path was barred. Then she said to them: -

"Hurry, children! The night comes when we cannot work!"

It was an hour of such good-will on earth to men that

no one could seem a stranger to her. He instantly became a human brother, next of kin to her - that was all; she was wholly under the influence of the innocence and purity within and without.

As he made no reply and for a moment did not move, she glanced quickly at him, regretting the smile. When she saw his face, he saw the joy go down out of hers; and he felt, as he turned off, that she went with him along the black street: alone, he seemed not alone any more.

Though he had been with her many times since, no later impression had effaced one line of that first picture. There she stood ever to him, and would stand: on the step of the church, smiling in her mourning, binding her wreath, the jets of the chandelier streaming out on her snow-sprinkled shoulder, the children carolling among the fragrant cedar boughs scattered at her feet; she there, decorating the church, happy to be of pious service. Ah, to have her there in the room with him now; to be able to turn his eyes to hers in the vanishing firelight, near sleep awaiting them, side by side.

There was the sound of a scratching on David's window shutters, as though a stiff brush were being moved up and down across the slats. He became aware that this sound had reached him at intervals several times already, but as often happens, had been disregarded by him owing to his preoccupation. Now it was so loud as to force itself positively upon his attention.

He listened, puzzled, wondering. His window stood high from the ground and clear of any object. In a few moments, the sound made itself audible again. He sprang up, wide awake now, and raising the sash, pushed open the shutters - one of them easily; against the other there was resistance from outside. This yielded before his pressure; and as the shutter was forced wide open and David peered out, there swung heavily against his cheek what felt like an enormous brush of thorns, covered with ice. It was the end of one of the limbs of the cedar tree which stood several feet from his window on one side, and close to the wall of the house. Before David was born, it had been growing there, a little higher, more far-reaching laterally, every year, until several topmost boughs had long since risen above the level of the eaves and dropped their dry needles on the rotting shingles. Now one of the limbs, bent over sidewise under its ice-freighted berries and twigs, hung as low as his window, and the wind was tossing it.

Sleet! This, then, was the nature of the threatening storm, which all day had made man and beast foreboding and distressed. David held out his hand: rain was falling steadily, each drop freezing on whatsoever it fell, adding ice to ice. The moon rode high by this time; and its radiance pouring from above on the roof of riftless cloud, diffused enough light below to render large objects near at hand visible in bulk and outline. A row of old cedars stretched across the yard. Their shapes, so familiar to him, were already disordered. The sleet must have been falling for hours to have weighed them down this way and that. A peculiarity of the night was the wind, which increased constantly, but with fitful violence, giving no warning of its high swoop, seizure, and wrench.

Sleet! Scarce a winter but he had seen some little:

once, in his childhood, a great one. He had often heard his father talk of others which HE remembered - with comment on the destruction they had wrought far and wide, on the suffering of all stock and of the wild creatures. The ravage had been more terrible in the forests, his father had thought, than what the cyclones cause when they rush upon the trees, heavy in their full summer-leaves, and sweep them down as easily as umbrellas set up on the ground. So much of the finest forests of Kentucky had been lost through its annual summer tempests and its rarer but more awful wintry sleets.

No work for him in the hemp fields to-morrow, nor for days. No school for Gabriella; the more distant children would be unable to ride; the nearest unable to foot it through the mirrored woods; unless the weather should moderate before morning and melt the ice away as quickly as it had formed - as sometimes was the case. A good sign of this, he took it, was the ever rising wind: for a rising wind and a falling temperature seldom appeared together. As he bent his ear listening, he could hear the wild roar of the surges of air breaking through the forest, the edge of which was not fifty yards away.

David sprang from his chair; there was a loud crack, and the great limb of the cedar swept rattling down across his shutters, twisted, snapped off at the trunk, rolled over in the air, and striking the ground on its back, lay like a huge animal knocked lifeless.

He forgot bed and sleep and replenished his fire. His ear, trained to catch and to distinguish sounds of country life, was now becoming alive to the commencement of one of those vast appalling catastrophes in

Nature, for which man sees no reason and can detect the furtherance of no plan - law being turned with seeming blindness, and in the spirit of sheer wastage, upon what it has itself achieved, and spending its sublime forces in a work of self-desolation.

Of the two windows in his room, one opened upon the back yard, one upon the front. Both back yard and front contained, according to the custom of the country, much shrubbery, with aged fruit trees, mostly cherry and peach. There were locusts also at the rear of the house, the old-time yard favorite of the people; other forest trees stood around. Through both his windows there began to reach him a succession of fragile sounds; the snapping of rotten, weakest, most overburdened twigs. On fruit tree and forest tree these went down first - as is also the law of storm and trial of strength among men. The ground was now as one flooring of glass; and as some of these small branches dropped from the tree-tops, they were broken into fragments, like icicles, and slid rattling away into the nearest depressions of the ground. Starting far up in the air sometimes, they struck sheer upon other lower branches, bringing them along also; this gathering weight in turn descended upon others lower yet, until, so augmented, the entire mass swept downward and fell, shivered against crystal flooring.

But soon these more trivial facts held his attention no longer: they were the mere reconnaissance of the elements - the first light attack of Nature upon her own weakness. By and by from the surging, roaring depths of the woods, there suddenly reverberated to him a deep boom as of a cannon: one of the great trees - two-forked at the mighty summit and already burdened in each half by its tons of timber, split in twain at the fork as though cleft by lightning; and now only the pointed trunk stood like a funeral shaft above its own ruins. For hours this went on: the light incessant rattling, closest around; the creaking, straining, tearing apart as of suffering flesh, less near; the sad, sublime booming of the forest.

Now the man would walk the floor; now drop into his chair before the fire. His last bit of candle flickered blue, deep in the socket, and sent up its smoke. His wood was soon burnt out: only red coals in the bottom of the grate then, and these fast whitening. More than once he strode across and stood over his trunk in the shadowy corner - looking down at his books - those books that had guided him thus far, or misguided him, who can say?

When his candle gave out and later his fire, he jerked off his clothes and getting into bed, rolled himself in the bedclothes and lay listening to the mournful sublimity of the storm.

Toward three o'clock the weather grew colder, the wind died down, the booming ceased; and David, turning wearily, over, with an impulse to prayer, but with no prayer, went to sleep.

XIV

When David awoke late and drowsily the next morning after the storm, he lay awhile, listening. No rending, crashing, booming in the woods now, nor rattling of his window-frames. No contemplative twitter of winter birds about the cedars in the yard, nor caw of crow, crossing the house chimneys toward the corn shocks. All things hushed, silent, immovable.

Following so quickly upon the sublime roar and ravage of the night before, the stillness was disturbing. He sprang up and dressed quickly - admonished by the coldness of his room - before hurrying to his window to look out. When he tried the sash, it could not be raised. He thrust his hand through the broken pane and tugged at the shutters; they could not be shaken. Running downstairs to the kitchen and returning with hot water, he melted away the ice embedding the bolts and hinges.

A marvel of nature, terrible, beautiful, met his eyes: ice-rain and a great frost Cloud, heavy still, but thinner than on the day before, enwrapped the earth. The sun, descending through this translucent roof of gray, filled the air beneath with a radiance as of molten pearl; and in this under-atmosphere of pearl all earthly things were tipped and hung in silver. Tree, bush, and shrub in the yard below, the rose clambering the pillars of the porch under his window, the scant ivy lower down on the house wall, the stiff little junipers, every blade of grass - all encased in silver. The ruined cedars trailed from sparlike tops their sweeping sails of incrusted emerald and silver. Along the eaves, like a row of inverted spears of unequal lengths, hung the argent icicles. No; not spun silver all this, but glass; all things buried, not under a tide of liquid silver, but of flowing and then cooling glass: Nature for once turned into a glass house, fixed in a brittle mass, nowhere bending or swaying; but if handled roughly, sure to be shivered.

The ground under every tree in the yard was strewn with boughs; what must be the ruin of the woods whence the noises had reached him in the night? Looking out of his window now, he could see enough to let him understand the havoc, the wreckage.

He went at once to the stable for the feeding and found everything strangely quiet - the stilling influence of a great frost on animal life. There had been excitement and uneasiness enough during the night; now ensued the reaction, for man is but one of the many animals with nerves and moods. A catastrophe like this which covers with ice the earth - grass, winter edible twig and leaf, roots and nuts for the brute kind that turns the soil with the nose, such putting of all food whatsoever out of reach of mouth or hoof or snout - brings these creatures face to face with the possibility of starving: they know it and are silent with apprehension of their peril; know it perhaps by the survival of prehistoric memories reverberating as instinct still. And there is another possible prong of truth to this repression of their characteristic cries at such times of frost: then it was in ages past that the species which preyed on them grew most ravenous and far ranging. The silence of the

James Lane Allen

modern stable in a way takes the place of that primeval silence which was a law of safety in the bleak fastnesses, hunted over by flesh eating prowlers. It is the prudent noiselessness of many a species to-day, as the deer and the moose.

The sheep, having enjoyed little shelter beside the hayrick, had encountered the worst of the storm. When David appeared in the stable lot, they beheld him at once; for their faces were bunched expectantly toward the yard gate through which he must emerge. But they spoke not a word to one another or to him as they hurried slipping forward. The man looked them over pityingly, yet with humor; for they wore many undesirable pendants of glass and silver dangling under their bellies and down their tails.

"You shall come into the barn this night," he vowed within himself. "I'll make a place for you this day."

Little did he foresee what awful significance to him lay wrapped in those simple words. Breakfast was ready when, carrying his customary basket of cobs for his mother, he returned to the house. One good result at least the storm had wrought for the time: it drew the members of the household more closely together, as any unusual event - danger, disaster - generally does. So that his father, despite his outburst of anger the night previous, forgot this morning his wrongs and disappointments and relaxed his severity. During the meal he had much to recount of other sleets and their consequences. He inferred similar consequences now if snow should follow, or a cold snap set in: no work in the fields, therefore no hemp-breaking, and therefore delay in selling the crop; the difficulty of feeding and watering the stock; no hauling along the mud roads, and little travel of any sort between country and town; the making of much cord wood out of the fallen timber, with plenty of stuff for woodpiles; the stopping of mill wheels on the frozen creeks, and scarcity of flour and meal.

"The meal is nearly out now," said David's mother. "The negroes waste it."

"We might shell some corn to-day," suggested David's father, hesitatingly. It was the first time since his son's return from college that he had ever proposed their working together.

"I'll take a look at the woods first," said David; "and then I want to make a place in the stable for the sheep, father. They must come under shelter to-night I'll fix new stalls for the horses inside where we used to have the corn crib. The cows can go where the horses have been, and the sheep can have the shed of the cows: it's better than nothing. I've been wanting to do this ever since I came home from college."

A thoughtless, unfortunate remark, as connected with that shabby, desperate idea of finding shelter for the stock - fresh reminder of the creeping, spreading poverty. His father made no rejoinder; and having finished his breakfast in silence, left the table.

His mother, looking across her coffeecup and biscuit at David, without change of expression inquired, -

"Will you get that hen?"

"WHAT hen, mother?"

"I told you last night the cook wanted one of the old hens for soup to-day. Will you get it?"

"No, mother; I will not get the hen for the cook; the cook will probably get the hen for me."

"She doesn't know the right one."

"But neither do I."

"I want the blue dorking."

"I have a bad eye for color; I might catch something gray."

"I want the dorking; she's stopped laying."

"Is that your motive for taking her life? It would be a terrible principle to apply indiscriminately!"

"The cook wants to know how she is to get the vegetables out of the holes in the garden to-day - under all this ice."

"How would she get the vegetables out of the garden under all this ice if there were no one on the place but herself? I warrant you she'd have every variety."

"It's a pity we are not able to hire a man. If we could hire a man to help her, I wouldn't ask you. It's hard on the cook, to make her suffer for our poverty."

"A little suffering in that way will do her a world of good," said David, cheerily.

His mother did not hesitate, provocation or no

provocation, to sting and reproach him in this way.

She had never thought very highly of her son; her disappointment, therefore, over his failure at college had not been keen. Besides, tragical suffering is the sublime privilege of deep natures: she escaped by smallness. Nothing would have made her very miserable but hunger and bodily pains. Against hunger she exercised ceaseless precautions; bodily pains she had none. The one other thing that could have agitated her profoundly was the idea that she would be compelled to leave Kentucky. It was hard for her to move about her house, much less move to Missouri. Not in months perhaps did she even go upstairs to bestow care upon, the closets, the bed, the comforts of her son. As might be expected, she considered herself the superior person of the family; and as often happens, she imposed this estimate of herself upon her husband. The terrifying vanity and self-sufficiency of the little-minded! Nature must set great store upon this type of human being, since it is regularly allowed to rule its betters.

But his father! David had been at home two months now, for this was the last of February, and not once during that long ordeal of daily living together had his father opened his lips either to reproach or question him.

Letters had been received from the faculty, from the pastor; of that David was aware; but any conversation as to these or as to the events of which they were the sad consummation, his father would not have. The gulf between them had been wide before; now it was fathomless.

James Lane Allen

Yet David well foreknew that the hour of reckoning had to come, when all that was being held back would be uttered. He realized that both were silently making preparations for that crisis, and that each day brought it palpably nearer. Sometimes he could even see it threatening in his father's eye, hear it in his voice. It had reached the verge of explosion the night previous, with that prediction of coming bankruptcy, the selling of the farm of his Kentucky ancestors, the removal to Missouri in his enfeebled health. Not until his return had David realized how literally his father had begun to build life anew on the hopes of him. And now feel with him in his disappointment as deeply as he might, sympathy he could not openly offer, explanation he could not possibly give. His life-problem was not his father's problem; his father was simply not in a position to understand. Doubt anything in the Bible - doubt so-called orthodox Christianity - be expelled from the church and from college for such a reason - where could his father find patience or mercy for wilful folly and impiety like that?

Meantime he had gone to work; on the very day after his return he had gone to work. Two sentences of his father's, on the afternoon of his coming home, had rung in David's ears loud and ceaselessly ever since: "WHY HAVE YOU COME BACK HERE?" And "I ALWAYS KNEW THERE WAS NOTHING IN YOU?" The first assured him of the new footing on which he stood: he was no longer desired under that roof. The second summed up the life-long estimate which had been formed of his character before he had gone away.

Therefore he had worked as never even in the old preparatory days. So long as he remained there, he must at least earn daily bread. More than that, he must make good, as soon as possible, the money spent at college. So he sent away the hired negro man; he undertook the work done by him and more: the care of the stock, the wood cutting, everything that a man can be required to do on a farm in winter. Of bright days he broke hemp. Nothing had touched David so deeply as the discovery in one corner of the farm of that field of hemp: his father had secretly raised it to be a surprise to him, to help him through his ministerial studies. This David had learned from his mother; his father had avoided mention of it: it might rot in the field! In equal silence David had set about breaking it; and sometimes at night his father would show enough interest merely to ask some questions regarding the day's work.

Yet, notwithstanding this impending tragedy with his father, and distress at their reduced circumstances caused by his expenses at college, David, during these two months, had entered into much new happiness.

The doubts which had racked him for many months were ended. He had reached a decision not to enter the ministry; had stripped his mind clean and clear of dogmas. The theologies of his day, vast, tangled thickets of thorns overspreading the simple footpath of the pious pilgrim mind, interfered with him no more. It was not now necessary for him to think or preach that any particular church with which he might identify himself was right, the rest of the human race wrong. He did not now have to believe that any soul was in danger of eternal damnation for disagreeing with him. Release from these things left his religious spirit more lofty and alive than ever.

For, moreover, David had set his feet a brief space on

the wide plains of living-knowledge; he had encountered through their works many of the great minds of his century, been reached by the sublime thought-movements of his time, heard the deep roar of the spirit's ocean. Amid coarse, daily labor once more, amid the penury and discord in that ruined farmhouse, one true secret of happiness with David was the recollection of all the noble things of human life which he had discovered, and to which he meant to work his way again as soon as possible. And what so helps one to believe in God as knowledge of the greatness of man?

Meantime, also, his mind was kept freshly and powerfully exercised. He had discarded his old way of looking at Nature and man's place in it; and of this fundamental change in him, no better proof could be given than the way in which he regarded the storm, as he left the breakfast-table this morning and went to the woods.

The damage was unreckonable. The trees had not been prepared against an event like that. For centuries some of them had developed strength in root and trunk and branch to resist the winds of the region when clad in all their leaves; or to carry the load of these leaves weighted with raindrops; or to bear the winter snows. Wise self-physicians of the forest! Removing a weak or useless limb, healing their own wounds and fractures! But to be buried under ice and then wrenched and twisted by the blast - for this they had received no training: and thus, like so many of the great prudent ones who look hourly to their well-being, they had been stricken down at last by the unexpected.

"Once," said David reverently to himself, beholding it

all, "once I should have seen in this storm some direct intention of the Creator toward man, even toward me. It would have been a reminder of His power; perhaps been a chastisement for some good end which I must believe in, but could not discover. Men certainly once interpreted storms as communications from the Almighty, as they did pestilence and famine. There still may be in this neighborhood people who will derive some such lesson from this. My father may in his heart believe it a judgment sent on us and on our neighbors for my impiety. Have not cities been afflicted on account of the presence of one sinner? Thankful I am not to think in this way now of physical law - not so to misconceive man's place in Nature. I know that this sleet, so important to us, is but one small incident in the long history of the planet's atmosphere and changing surface. It is the action of natural laws, operating without regard to man, though man himself may have had a share in producing it. It will bring death to many a creature; indirectly, it may bring death to me; but that would be among the results, not in the intention."

He set his face to cross the wood - sliding, skating, steadying himself against the trunks, driving his heels through the ice crust The exercise was heating; his breath rose as a steam before his face. Beyond the woods he crossed a field; then a forest of many acres and magnificent timber, on the far edge of which, under the forest trees and fronting a country lane, stood the schoolhouse of the district. David looked anxiously, as he drew near, for any signs of injury that the storm might have done. One enormous tree-top had fallen on the fence. A limb had dropped sheer on the steps. The entire yard was little better than a brush heap. He soon turned away home relieved: he would be able to tell Gabriella to-night that none of the windows had been broken nor the roof; only a new woods scholar, with little feet and a big hard head and a bunch of mistletoe in one hand, was standing on the steps, waiting for her to open the door.

David's college experience had effected the first great change in him as he passed from youth to manhood; Gabriella had wrought the second. The former was a fragment of the drama of man's soul with God; the latter was the drama of his heart with woman.

It had begun the day the former ended - in the gloom of that winter twilight day, when he had quit the college after his final interview with the faculty, and had wandered forlorn and dazed into the happy town, just commencing to celebrate its season of peace on earth and good will to man. He had found her given up heart and soul to the work of decorating the church of her faith, the church of her fathers.

When David met her the second time, it was a few days after his return home. He was at work in the smoke-house. The meat had been salted down long enough after the killing: it must be hung, and he was engaged in hanging it. Several pieces lay piled inside the door suitably for the hand. He stood with his back to these beside the meat bench, scraping the saltpetre off a large middling and rubbing it with red pepper. Suddenly the light of the small doorway failed; and turning he beheld his mother, and a few feet behind her - David said that he did not believe in miracles - but a few feet behind his mother there now stood a divine presence. Believe it or not, there she was, the miracle! All the bashfulness of his lifetime - it had often made existence well-nigh insupportable - came crowding into that one moment. The feeblest little bleat of a spring lamb too weak to stand up for the first time would have been a deafening roar in comparison with the silence which now penetrated to the marrow of his bones. He faced the two women at bay, with one hand resting on the middling.

"This is my son," said his mother neutrally, turning to the young lady. This information did not help David at all. He knew who HE was. He took it for granted that every one present knew. The visitor at once relieved the situation.

"This is the school-teacher," she said, coloring and smiling. "I have been teaching here ever since you went away. And I am now an old resident of this neighborhood."

Not a thing moved about David except a little smoke in the chimney of his throat. But the young lady did not wait for more silence to render things more tense. She stepped forward into the doorway beside his mother and peered curiously in, looking up at the smoke-blackened joists, at the black cross sticks on which the links of sausages were hung, at the little heap of gray ashes in the ground underneath with a ring of half-burnt chips around them, at the huge meat bench piled with salted joints.

"And this is the way you make middlings?" she inquired, smiling at him encouragingly.

The idea of that archangel knowing anything about middlings! David's mind executed a rudimentary movement, and his tongue and lips responded feebly: -

"This is the way."

"And this is the way you make hams, sugar-cured hams?"

"This is the way."

"And this is the way you make - shoulders?"

"This is the way."

David had found an answer, and he was going to abide by it while strength and daylight lasted.

The young lady seemed to perceive that this was his intention.

"Let me see you HANG one," she said desperately. "I have never seen bacon hanged - or hung. I suppose as I teach grammar, I must use both participles."

David caught up the huge middling by the string and swung it around in front of him, whereupon it slipped out of his nerveless fingers and fell over in the ashes. It did not break the middling, but it broke the ice.

"Can I help you?"

Those torturing, blistering words! David's face got as red as though it had been rubbed with red pepper and saltpetre both. The flame of it seemed to kindle some faint spark of spirit in him. He picked up the middling, and as he looked her squarely in the eye, with a humorous light in his, he nodded at the pieces of bacon by the entrance.

"Hang one of those," he said, "if you've a mind."

As he lifted the middling high, Gabriella noticed above his big red hands a pair of arms like marble for lustre and whiteness (for he had his sleeves rolled far back) - as massive a pair of man's arms as ever were formed by life-long health and a life-long labor and life-long right living.

"Thank you," she said, retreating through the door. "It's all very interesting. I have never lived in the country before. Your mother told me you were working here, and I asked her to let me come and look on. While I have been living in your neighborhood, you have been living in my town. I hope you will come to see me, and tell me a great deal."

As she said this, David perceived that she, standing behind his mother, looked at him with the veiled intention of saying far more. He had such an instinct for truth himself, that truth in others was bare to him. Those gentle, sympathetic eyes seemed to declare: "I know about your troubles. I am the person for whom, without knowing it, you have been looking. With me you can break silence about the great things. We can meet far above the level of such poor scenes as this. I have sought you to tell you this. Come."

"Mother," said David that evening, after his father had left the table, dropping his knife and fork and forgetting to eat, "who was that?"

He drew out all that could be drawn: that she had come to take charge of the school the autumn he had gone away; that she was liked as a teacher, liked by the old people. She had taken great interest in HIM, his mother said reproachfully, and the idea of his studying for the ministry. She had often visited the house, had been good to his father and to her. This was her first visit since she had gotten back; she had been in town spending the holidays.

David had begun to go to see Gabriella within a week. At first he went once a week - on Saturday nights. Soon he went twice a week - Wednesdays and Saturdays invariably. On that last day at college, when he had spoken out for himself, he had ended the student and the youth; when he met her, it was the beginning of the man: and the new reason of the man's happiness.

As he now returned home across the mile or more of country, having satisfied himself as to the uninjured condition of the schoolhouse, which had a great deal to do with Gabriella's remaining in that neighborhood, he renewed his resolve to go to see her to-night, though it was only Friday. Had not the storm upset all regular laws and customs?

Happily, then, on reaching the stable, he fell to work upon his plan of providing a shelter for the sheep.

David felt much more at home in the barn than at the house. For the stock saw no change in him. Believer or unbeliever, rationalist, evolutionist, he was still the same to them. Upon them, in reality, fell the ill consequences of his misspent or well-spent college life; for the money which might have gone for shingles and joists and more provender, had in part been spent on books describing the fauna of the earth and the distribution of species on its surface. Some had gone for treatises on animals under domestication, while his own animals under domestication were allowed to go poorly fed and worse housed. He had had the theory; they had had the practice. But they apprehended nothing of all this. How many tragedies of evil passion brutes escape by not understanding their owners! We of the human species so often regret that individuals read each other's natures so dimly: let us be thankful! David was glad, then, that this little aggregation of dependent creatures, his congregation of the faithful, neither perceived the change in him, nor were kept in suspense by the tragedy growing at the house.

They had been glad to see him on his return. Captain, who had met him first, was gladdest, perhaps. Then the horses, the same old ones. One of them, he fancied, had backed up to him, offering a ride. And the cows were friendly. They were the same; their calves were different. The sheep about maintained their number, their increase by nature nearly balancing their decrease by table use.

One member of the flock David looked for in vain: the boldest, gentlest - there usually is one such. Later on he found it represented by a saddle blanket. After his departure for college, his mother had conceived of this fine young wether in terms of sweetbreads, tallow for chapped noses, and a soft seat for the spine of her husband. Even the larded dame of the snow-white sucklings had remembered him well, and had touched her snout against his boots; so that hardly had he in the old way begun to stroke her bristles, before she spoke comfortably of her joy, and rolled heavily over in what looked like a grateful swoon.

No: his animals had not changed in their feelings toward him; but how altered he in his understanding of them! He had formerly believed that these creatures were created for the use of man - that old conceited notion that the entire earth was a planet of provisions for human consumption. It had never even occurred to him to think that the horses were made but to ride and to work. Cows of course gave milk for the sake of the dairy; cream rose on milk for ease in skimming; when churned, it turned sour, that the family might have fresh buttermilk. Hides were for shoes. The skin on sheep, it was put there for Man's woollens.

Now David declared that these beings were no more made for Man than Man was made for them. Man might capture them, keep them in captivity, break, train, use, devour them, occasionally exterminate them by benevolent assimilation. But this was not the reason of their being created: what that reason was in the Creator's mind, no one knew or would ever know.

"Man seizes and uses you," said David, working that day in his barn; "but you are no more his than he is yours. He calls you dependent creatures: who has made you dependent? In a state of wild nature, there is not one of you that Man would dare meet: not the wild stallion, not the wild bull, not the wild boar, not even an angry ram. The argument that Man's whole physical constitution - structure and function-shows that he was intended to live on beef and mutton, is no better than the argument that the tiger finds man perfectly adapted to his system as a food, and desires none better. Every man-eating creature thinks the same: the wolf believes Man to be his prey; the crocodile believes him to be his; an old lion is probably sure that a man's young wife is designed for his maw alone. So she is, if he manages to catch her."

As David said this rather unexpectedly to himself, he fell into a novel revery, forgetting philosophy and brute kind. It was late when David finished his work that day. Toward nightfall the cloud had parted in the west; the sun had gone down with dark curtains closing heavily over it. Later, the cloud had parted in the east, and the moon had arisen amid white fleeces and floated above banks of pearl. Shining upon all splendid things else, it illumined one poor scene which must not be forgotten: the rear of an old barn, a sagging roof of rotting shingles; a few common sheep passing in, driven by a shepherd dog; and a big thoughtful boy holding the door open.

He had shifted the stock to make way for these additional pensioners, putting the horses into the new stalls, the cows where the horses had been, and the sheep under the shed of the cows. (It is the horse that always gets the best of everything in a stable.) He reproached himself that he did least for the creatures that demanded least

"That's the nature of man," he said disapprovingly, "topmost of all brutes."

When he stepped out of doors after supper that night, the clouds had hidden the moon. But there was light enough for him to see his way across the ice fields to Gabriella. The Star of Love shone about his feet.

XV

When Gabriella awoke on that same morning after the storm, she too ascertained that her shutters could not be opened. But Gabriella did not go down into the kitchen for hot water to melt the ice from the bolts and hinges. She fled back across the cold matting to the high-posted big bed and cuddled down solitary into its warmth again, tucking the counterpane under her chin and looking out from the pillows with eyes as fresh as flowers. Flowers in truth Gabriella's eyes were - the closing and disclosing blossoms of a sweet nature. Somehow they made you think of earliest spring, of young leaves, of the flutings of birds deep within a glade sifted with golden light, fragrant with white fragrance. They had their other seasons: their summer hours of angry flash and swift downpour; their autumn days of still depths and soberness, and autumn nights of long, quiet rainfalls when no one knew. One season they lacked: Gabriella's eyes had no winter,

Brave spirit! Had nature not inclined her to spring rather than autumn, had she not inherited joyousness and the temperamental gayety of the well-born, she must long ago have failed, broken down. Behind her were generations of fathers and mothers who had laughed heartily all their days. The simple gift of wholesome laughter, often the best as often the only remedy for so many discomforts and absurdities in life - this was perhaps to be accounted among her best psychological heirlooms.

Her first thought on awaking late this morning (for she too had been kept awake by the storm) was that there could be no school. And this was only Friday, with Saturday and Sunday to follow - three whole consecutive days of holiday! Gabriella's spirits invariably rose in a storm; her darkest days were her brightest. The weather that tried her soul was the weather which was disagreeable, but not disagreeable enough to break up school. When she taught, she taught with all her powers and did it well; when not teaching, she hated it with every faculty and capacity of her being. And to discharge patiently and thoroughly a daily hated work - that takes noble blood.

Nothing in the household stirred below. The members of the family had remained up far into the night. As for the negroes, they understand how to get a certain profit for themselves out of all disturbances of the weather. Gabriella was glad of the chance to wait for the house-girl to come up and kindle her fire - grateful for the luxury of lying in bed on Friday morning, instead of getting up to a farmer's early breakfast, when sometimes there were candles on the table to reveal the localities of the food! How she hated those candles, flaring in her eyes so early! How she loved the mellow flicker of them at night, and how she hated them in the morning - those early-breakfast candles!

In high spirits, then, with the certainty of a late breakfast and no school, she now lay on the pillows, looking across with sparkling eyes at last night's little gray ridge of ashes under the bars of her small grate. Those hearthstones! - when her bare soles accidentally touched one on winter mornings, Gabriella was of the opinion that they were the coldest bricks that ever came from a fiery furnace. There was one thing in the room still colder: the little cherrywood washstand away over on the other side of the big room between the windows, - placed there at the greatest possible distance from the fire! Sometimes when she peeped down into her wash-pitcher of mornings, the ice bulged up at her like a white cannon-ball that had gotten lodged on the way out. She jabbed at it with the handle of her toothbrush; or, if her temper got the best of her (or the worst), with the poker. Often her last act at night was to dry her toothbrush over the embers so that the hair in it would not be frozen in the morning.

Gabriella raised her head from the pillows and peeped over at the counterpane covering her. It consisted of stripes of different colors, starting from a point at the middle of the structure and widening toward the four sides. Her feet were tucked away under a bank of plum color sprinkled with salt; up her back ran a sort of comet's tail of puddled green. Over her shoulder and descending toward her chin, flowed a broadening delta of well-beaten egg.

She was thankful for these colors. The favorite hue of the farmer's wife was lead. Those hearthstones - lead! The strip of oilcloth covering the washstand - lead! The closet in the wall containing her things - lead! The stair-steps outside - lead! The porches down below - lead! Gabriella sometimes wondered whether this woman might not have had lead-colored ancestors.

A pair of recalcitrant feet were now heard mounting the stair: the flowers on the pillow closed their petals. When the negro girl knelt down before the grate, with her back to the bed and the soles of her shoes set up straight side by side like two gray bricks, the eyes were softly opened again, Gabriella had never seen a head like this negro girl's, that is, never until the autumn before last, when she had come out into this neighborhood of plain farming people to teach a district school. Whenever she was awake early enough to see this curiosity, she never failed to renew her study of it with unflagging zest. It was such a mysterious, careful arrangement of knots, and pine cones, and the strangest-looking little black sticks wrapped with white packing thread, and the whole system of coils seemingly connected with a central mental battery, or idea, or plan, within. She studied it now, as the fire was being kindled, and the kindler, with inflammatory blows of the poker on the bars of the grate, told her troubles over audibly to herself: "Set free, and still making fires of winter mornings; how was THAT? Where was any freedom in THAT? Her wages? Didn't she work for her wages? Didn't she EARN her wages? Then where did freedom come in?"

One must look low for high truth sometimes, as we gather necessary fruit on nethermost boughs and dig the dirt for treasure. The Anglo-Saxon girl lying in the bed and the young African girl kindling her fire - these two, the highest and the humblest types of womanhood in the American republic - were inseparably connected in that room that morning as children of the same Revolution. It had cost the war of the Union, to enable this African girl to cast away the cloth enveloping her head - that detested sign of her slavery - and to arrange her hair with ancestral taste, the true African beauty sense. As long as she had been a slave, she had been compelled by her Anglo-Saxon mistress to wear her head-handkerchief; as soon as she was set free, she, with all the women of her race in the South, tore the head-handkerchief indignantly off. In the same way, it cost the war of the Union to enable Gabriella to teach school. She had been set free also, and the bandage removed from her liberties. The negress had been empowered to demand wages for her toil; the Anglo-Saxon girl had been empowered to accept without reproach the wages for hers.

Gabriella's memoirs might be writ large in four parts that would really be the history of the United States, just as a slender seam of gold can only be explained through the geology of the earth. But they can also be writ so small that each volume may be dropped, like certain minute-books of bygone fashions, into a waistcoat pocket, or even read, as through a magnifying glass, entire on a single page.

The first volume was the childhood book, covering the period from Gabriella's birth to the beginning of the Civil War, by which time she was fourteen years old: it was fairy tale. These earliest recollections went back to herself as a very tiny child living with her mother and grandmother in a big white house with green window-shutters, in Lexington - so big that she knew only the two or three rooms in one ell. Her mother wore mourning for her father, and was always drawing her to her bosom and leaving tears on her face or lilylike hands. One day - she could not remember very well - but the house had been darkened and the servants never for a moment ceased amusing her - one day the house was all opened again and Gabriella could not find her mother; and her grandmother, everybody else, was kinder to her than ever. She did not think what kindness was then, but years afterward she learned perfectly.

Very slowly Gabriella's knowledge began to extend over the house and outside it. There were enormous, high-ceiled halls and parlors, and bedrooms and bedrooms and bedrooms. There were verandas front and back, so long that it took her breath away to run the length of one and return. Upstairs, front and back, verandas again, balustraded so that little girls could not forget themselves and fall off. The pillars of these verandas at the rear of the house were connected by a network of wires, and trained up the pillars and branching over the wires were coiling twisting vines of wisteria as large as Gabriella's neck. This was the sunny southern side; and when the wisteria was blooming, Gabriella moved her establishment of playthings out behind those sunlit cascades of purple and green, musical sometimes with goldfinches.

The front of the house faced a yard of stately evergreens and great tubs of flowers, oleander, crepe myrtle, and pomegranate. Beyond the yard, a gravelled carriage drive wound out of sight behind cedars, catalpa, and forest trees, shadowing a turfy lawn. At the end of the lawn was the great entrance gate and the street of the town, Gabriella long knew this approach only by her drives with her grandmother. At the rear of the house was enough for her: a large yard, green grazing lots for the stable of horses, and best of all a high-fenced garden containing everything the heart could desire: vegetables, and flowers; summer-houses, and arbors with seats; pumps of cold water, and hot-houses of plants and grapes, and fruit trees, and a swing, and gooseberry bushes - everything.

In one corner, the ground was too shaded by an old apple tree to be of use: they gave this to Gabriella for her garden. She had attached particularly to her person a little negress of about the same age - her Milly, the color of a ripe gourd. So when in spring the gardener began to make his garden, with her grandmother sometimes standing over him, directing, Gabriella, taking her little chair to the apple tree, - with some pretended needle-work and a real switch, - would set Milly to work making hers. Nothing that they put into the earth ever was heard of again, though they would sometimes make the same garden over every day for a week. So that more than once, forsaking seed, they pulled off the tops of green things near by, planted these, and so had a perfect garden in an hour.

Then Gabriella, seated under the apple tree, would order Milly to water the flowers from the pump; and taking her switch and calling Milly close, she would give her a sharp rap or two around the bare legs (for that was expected), and tell her that if she didn't stop being so trifling, she would sell her South to the plantations. Whereupon Milly, injured more in heart than legs, and dropping the watering-pot, would begin to bore her dirty fists into her eyes. Then Gabriella would say repentantly: -

"No, I won't, Milly! And you needn't work any more to-day. And you can have part of my garden if you want it."

Milly, smiling across the mud on her cheeks, would murmur: -

"You ain' goin' sell yo' Milly down South, is you, Miss Gabriella?"

"*I* won't. But I'm not so sure about grandmother, Milly. You know she WILL do it sometimes. Our cotton's got to be picked by SOMEBODY, and who's to do it but you lazy negroes?"

In those days the apple tree would be blooming, and the petals would sift down on Gabriella. Looking up at the marriage bell of blossoms, and speaking in the language of her grandmother, she would say: -

"Milly, when I grow up and get married, I am going to be married out of doors in spring under an apple tree."

"I don' know whah *I* gwine be married," Milly would say with a hoarse, careless cackle. "I 'spec' in a brier-patch."

Gabriella's first discovery of what meanness human nature can exhibit was connected with this garden. So long as everything was sour and green, she could play there by the hour; but as soon as anything got ripe and delicious, the gate with the high latch was shut and she could never enter it unguarded. What tears she shed outside the fence as she peeped through! When they did take her in, they always held her by the hand.

"DON'T hold my hand, Sam," pleadingly to the negro gardener. "It's so HOT!"

"You fall down and hurt yourself."

"How absurd, Sam! The idea of my falling down when I am walking along slowly!"

"You get lost."

"How can you say anything so amusing as that, Sam! Did I ever get lost in here?"

"Snakes bite you."

"Why do you think they'd bite ME, Sam? They have never been known to bite anybody else."

"You scratch yourself."

"How can I scratch myself, Sam, when I'm not doing anything?"

"Caterpillars crawl on you."

"They crawl on me when I'm not in the garden, Sam. So why do you harp on THAT?"

Slowly they walked on - past the temptations of Eden.

"Please, let me try just once, Sam!"

"Try what, Miss Gabriella?"

"To see whether the snakes will bite me."

"I couldn't!"

"Then take me to see the grapes," she would say wearily.

There they were, hanging under the glass: bunches of black and of purple Hamburgs, and of translucent Malagas, big enough to have been an armful!

"Just one, Sam, please."

"Make you sick."

"They never make me sick when I eat them in the house. They are good for me! One COULDN'T make me sick. I'm sick because you DON'T give it to me. Don't I LOOK sick, Sam?"

The time came when Gabriella began to extend her knowledge to the country, as she drove out beside her grandmother in the balmy spring and early summer afternoons.

"What is that, grandmother?" she would say, pointing with her small forefinger to a field by the turnpike.

"That is corn."

"And what is that?"

"That is wheat."

"And what is that?"

"Oats, Gabriella."

"Oh, grandmother, what is THAT?"

"Tut, tut, child! Don't you know what that is? That's hemp. That is what bales all our cotton."

"Oh, grandmother, smell it!"

After this sometimes Gabriella would order the driver to turn off into some green lane about sunset and press on till they found a field by the way. As soon as they began to pass it, over into their faces would be wafted the clean, cooling, velvet-soft, balsam breath of the hemp. The carriage would stop, and Gabriella, standing up and facing the field, would fill her lungs again and again, smiling at her grandmother for approval. Then she would take her seat and say quietly: -

"Turn round, Tom, and drive back. I have smelt it enough."

These drives alone with her grandmother were for spring and early summer only. Full summer brought up from their plantations in Louisiana, Arkansas, and Mississippi, her uncles and the wives and children of some of them. All the bedrooms in the big house were filled, and Gabriella was nearly lost in the multitude, she being the only child of the only daughter of her grandmother. And now what happy times there were. The silks, and satins, and laces! The plate, the gold, the cut glass! The dinners, the music, the laughter, the wines!

Later, some of her uncles' families might travel on with their servants to watering places farther north. But in September all were back again under the one broad Kentucky roof, stopping for the beautiful Lexington fair, then celebrated all over the land; and for the races - those days of the thoroughbred only; and until frost fall should make it safe to return to the swamps and bayous, loved by the yellow fever.

When all were departed, sometimes her grandmother, closing the house for the winter, would follow one of her sons to his plantation; thence later proceeding to New Orleans, at that time the most brilliant of American capitals; and so Gabriella would see the Father of Waters, and the things that happened in the floating palaces of the Mississippi; see the social life of the ancient French and Spanish city.

All that could be most luxurious and splendid in Kentucky during those last deep, rich years of the old social order, was Gabriella's: the extravagance, the gayety, the pride, the lovely manners, the selfishness and cruelty in its terrible, unconscious, and narrow way, the false ideals, the aristocratic virtues. Then it was that, overspreading land and people, lay the full autumn of that sowing, which had moved silently on its way toward its fateful fruits for over fifty years. Everything was ripe, sweet, mellow, dropping, turning rotten.

O ye who have young children, if possible give them happy memories! Fill their earliest years with bright pictures! A great historian many centuries ago wrote it down that the first thing conquered in battle are the eyes: the soldier flees from what he sees before him. But so often in the world's fight we are defeated by what we look back upon; we are whipped in the end by the things we saw in the beginning of life. The time arrived for Gabriella when the gorgeous fairy tale of her childhood was all that she had to sustain her: when it meant consolation, courage, fortitude, victory.

A war volume, black, fiery, furious, awful - this comprised the second part of her history: it contained the overthrow of half the American people, and the downfall of the child princess Gabriella. An idea - how negative, nerveless, it looks printed! A little group of four ideas - how should they have power of life and death over millions of human beings! But say that one is the idea of the right of self-government - much loved and fought for all round the earth by the Anglo-Saxon race. Say that a second is the idea that with his own property a man has a right to do as he pleases: another notion that has been warred over, world without end. Let these two ideas run in the blood and passions of the Southern people. Say that a third idea is that of national greatness (the preservation of the Union), another idol of this nation-building race. Say that the fourth idea is that of evolving humanity, or, at least, that slave-holding societies must be made non-slave-holding - if not peaceably, then by force of arms. Let these two ideas be running in the blood and passions of the Northern people. Bring the first set of ideas and the second set together in a struggle for supremacy. By all mankind it is now known what the result was for the nation. What these ideas did for one little girl, living in Lexington, Kentucky, was part of that same sad, sublime history.

They ordered the grandmother across the lines, as a wealthy sympathizer and political agent of the Southern cause; they seized her house, confiscated it, used it as officers' headquarters: in the end they killed her with grief and care; they sent her sons, every man of them, into the Southern armies, ravaged their plantations, liberated their slaves, left them dead on the fields of battle, or wrecked in health, hope, fortune. Gabriella, placed in a boarding-school in Lexington at that last hurried parting with her grandmother, stayed there a year. Then the funds left to her account in bank were gone; she went to live with near relatives; and during the remaining years of the war was first in one household, then another, of kindred or friends all of whom contended for the privilege of finding her a home. But at the close of the war, Gabriella, issuing from the temporary shelters given her during the storm, might have been seen as a snow-white pigeon flying lost and bewildered across a black cloud covering half the sky.

The third volume - the Peace Book in which there was no Peace: this was the beginning of Gabriella, child of the Revolution. She did not now own a human being except herself; could give orders to none but herself; could train for this work, whip up to that duty, only herself; and if, she was still minded to play the mistress - firm, kind, efficient, capable - must be such a mistress solely to Gabriella.

By that social evolution of the race which in one country after another had wrought the overthrow of slavery, she had now been placed with a generation unique in history: a generation of young Southern girls, of gentle birth and breeding, of the most delicate nature, who, heiresses in slaves and lands at the beginning of the war, were penniless and unrecognized wards of the federal government at its close, their slaves having been made citizens and their plantations laid waste. On these unprepared and innocent girls thus fell most heavily not only the mistakes and misdeeds of their own fathers and mothers but the common guilt of the whole nation, and particularly of New England, as respects the original traffic in human souls. The change in the lives of these girls was as sudden and terrible as if one had entered a brilliant ballroom and in the voice of an overseer ordered the dancers to go as they were to the factories.

To the factories many of them went, in a sense: to hard work of some sort - to wage-earning and wage-taking: sometimes becoming the mainstay of aged or infirm parents, the dependence of younger brothers and sisters. If the history of it all is ever written, it will make pitiful, heroic, noble reading.

The last volume of Gabriella's memoirs showed her in this field of struggle - of new growth to suit the newer day. It was so unlike the first volume as to seem no continuation of her own life. It began one summer morning about two years after the close of the war - an interval which she had spent in various efforts at self-help, at self-training.

On that morning, pale and trembling, but resolute, her face heavily veiled, she might have been seen on her way to Water Street in Lexington - a street she had heard of all her life and had been careful never to enter except to take or to alight from a train at the station. Passing quickly along until she reached a certain ill-smelling little stairway which opened on the foul sidewalk, she mounted it, knocked at a low black-painted plank door, and entered a room which was a curiosity shop. There she was greeted by an elderly gentleman, who united in himself the offices of superintendent of schools, experimental astronomer, and manufacturer of a high grade of mustard. She had presented herself to be examined for a teacher's certificate.

Fortunately for Gabriella this kindly old sage remembered well her grandmother and her uncles: they had been connoisseurs; they had for years bought liberally of his mustard. Her uncles had used it first on their dinner tables as a condiment and afterward on their foreheads and stomachs as a plaster. They had never failed to praise it to his face - both for its power to draw an appetite and for its power to withdraw an ache. In turn he now praised them and asked the easiest questions. Gabriella, whose knowledge of arithmetic was as a grain of mustard seed, and who spoke beautiful English, but could not have parsed, "John, come here!" - received a first-class certificate for the sake of the future and a box of mustard in memory of the past.

Early in that autumn she climbed, one morning, into an old yellow-red, ever muddied stage-coach (the same that David had ridden in) and set out to a remote neighborhood, where, after many failures otherwise, she had secured a position to teach a small country school. She was glad that it was distant; she had a feeling that the farther away it was from Lexington, the easier it would be to teach.

Nearly all that interminable day, the mechanism of the stage and the condition of the pike (much fresh-cracked limestone on it) administered to Gabriella's body such a massage as is not now known to medical science. But even this was as nothing in comparison to the rack on which she stretched every muscle of her mind. What did she know about teaching? What kind of people would they be?

Late that mild September afternoon she began to find out The stage stopped at the mouth of a lane; and looking out with deathly faintness, Gabriella saw, standing beside a narrow, no-top buggy, a big, hearty, sunburned farmer with his waist-coat half unbuttoned, wearing a suit of butternut jeans and a yellow straw hat with the wide brim turned up like a cow's horns.

"Have you got my school-teacher in there?" he called out in a voice that carried like a heavy, sweet-sounding bell. "And did you bring me them things I told you to get?"

"Which is she?" he asked as he came over to the stage

window and peered in at the several travellers.

"How do you do, Miss Gabriella?" he said, taking his hat clear off his big, honest, hairy, brown head and putting in a hand that would have held several of Gabriella's. "I'm glad to see you; and the children have been crying for you. Now, if you will just let me help you to a seat in the buggy, and hold the lines for a minute while I get some things Joe's brought me, we'll jog along home. I'm glad to see you. I been hearing a heap about you from the superintendent."

Gabriella already loved him! When they were seated in the buggy, he took up six-sevenths of the space. She was so close to him that it scared her - so close that when he turned his head on his short, thick neck to look at her, he could hardly see her.

"He has a little slip of a wife," explained Gabriella to herself. "I'm in her seat: that's why he's used to it."

So SHE got used to it; and soon felt a frank comfort in being able to nestle freely against him - to cling to him like a bat to a warm wall. For cling sometimes she must. He was driving a sorrel fresh from pasture, with long, ragged hoofs, burrs in mane and tail, and a wild desire to get home to her foal; so that she fled across the country - bridges, ditches, everything, frantic with maternal passion. One circumstance made for Gabriella's security: the buggy tilted over toward him so low, that she could not conveniently roll out: instead she felt as though she were being whirled around a steep hillside.

Meantime, how he talked to her! Told her the school was all made up: what families were going to send, and how many children from each. They had all heard from the superintendent what a fine teacher she was (not for nothing is it said that things are handed along kindly in Kentucky)!

"Oh," murmured Gabriella to herself, "if the family are only like HIM!" The mere way in which he called her by her first name, as though she were an old friend - a sort of old sweetheart of his whom for some reason he had failed to marry - filled her with perfect trust.

"That's my house!" he said at last, pointing with extended arm and whip (which latter he had no occasion to use) across the open country.

Gabriella followed his gesture with apprehensive eyes and beheld away off a big comfortable-looking two-story brick dwelling with white-washed fences around it and all sorts of white-washed houses on one side or the other - a plain, sweet, country, Kentucky home, God bless it! The whiteness won Gabriella at once; and with the whiteness went other things just as good: the assurance everywhere of thrift, comfort. Not a weed in sight, but September bluegrass, deep flowing, or fresh-ploughed fields or clean stubble. Every rail in its place on every fence; every gate well swung. Everything in sight in the way of live stock seemed to Gabriella either young or just old enough. The very stumps they passed looked healthy.

Her conjecture had been correct: the slender slip of a woman met her at the side porch a little diffidently, with a modest smile; then kissed her on the mouth and invited her in. The supper table was already set in the middle of the room; and over in one corner was a big white bed - with a trundle bed (not visible) under it.

James Lane Allen

Gabriella "took off her things" and laid them on the snowy counterpane; and the housewife told her she would let the children entertain her for a few minutes while she saw about supper.

The children accepted the agreement. They swarmed about her as about a new cake. Two or three of the youngest began to climb over her as they climbed over the ice-house, to sit on her as they sat on the stiles. The oldest produced their geographies and arithmetics and showed her how far they had gone. (They had gone a great deal farther than Gabriella!) No one paid the least attention to any one else, or stood in awe of anything or anybody: Fear had never come to that Jungle!

But trouble must enter into the affairs of this world, and it entered that night into Gabriella.

At supper the farmer, having picked out for her the best piece of the breast of the fried chicken, inquired in a voice which implied how cordially superfluous the question was: -

"Miss Gabriella, will you have cream gravy?"

"No, thank you."

The shock to that family! Not take cream gravy! What kind of a teacher was that, now? Every small hand, old enough to use a knife or fork, held it suspended. At the foot of the table, the farmer, dropping his head a little, helped the children, calling their names one by one, more softly and in a tone meant to restore cheerfulness if possible. The little wife at the head of the table had just put sugar into Gabriella's cup and was in the act of pouring the coffee. She hastily emptied the sugar back into the sugar-dish and asked with look of dismay: -

"Will you have sugar in your coffee?"

The situation grew worse at breakfast. In a voice to which confidence had been mysteriously restored during the night - a voice that seemed to issue from a honey-comb and to drip sweetness all the way across the table, that big fellow at the foot again inquired: -

"Miss Gabriella, will you have cream gravy - THIS MORNING?"

"No, thank you!"

The oldest boy cocked his eye sideways at his mother, openly announcing that he had won a secret wager. The mother hastily remarked: -

"I thought you might like a little for your breakfast."

The baby, noticing the stillness and trouble every-where, and feeling itself deeply wounded because perfectly innocent, burst into frantic crying.

Gabriella could have outcried the baby! She resolved that if they had it for dinner, she would take it though it were the dessert. A moment later she did better. Lifting her plate in both hands, she held it out, knife, fork, and all.

"I believe I'll change my mind. It looks SO tempting."

"I think you'll find it nice," remarked the housewife, conciliated, but resentful. But every child now determined to watch and see what else she didn't take.

They watched in vain: she took everything. So that in a few days they recovered their faith in her and resumed their crawling. Gabriella had never herself realized how many different routes and stations she had in her own body until it had been thus travelled over: feet and ankles; knees; upper joints; trunk line; eastern and western divisions; head terminal.

There was never any more trouble for her in that household. They made only two demands: that she eat whatever was put on the table and love them. Whatever was put on the table was good; and they were all lovable. They were one live, disorderly menagerie of nothing but love. But love is not the only essential of life; and its phenomena can be trying.

Here, then, in this remote neighborhood of plain farmers, in a little district school situated on a mud road, Gabriella began alone and without training her new life, - attempt of the Southern girl to make herself self-supporting in some one of the professions, - sign of a vast national movement among the women of her people. In her surroundings and ensuing struggles she had much use for that saving sense of humor which had been poured into her veins out of the deep clear wells of her ancestors; need also of that radiant, bountiful light which still fell upon her from the skies of the past; but more than these as staff to her young hands, cup to her lips, lamp to her feet, oil to her daily bruises, rest to her weary pillow, was reliance on Higher Help. For the years - and they seemed to her many and wide - had already driven Gabriella, as they have driven countless others of her sex, out of the cold, windy world into the church: she had become a Protestant devotee. Had she been a Romanist, she would long ere this have been a nun. She was now fitted for any of those merciful and heroic services which keep fresh on earth the records of devoted women. The inner supporting stem of her nature had never been snapped; but it had been bruised enough to give off life-fragrance. Adversity had ennobled her. In truth, she had so weathered the years of a Revolution which had left her as destitute as it had left her free, that she was like Perdita's rosemary: a flower which keeps seeming and savor all the winter long. The North Wind had bolted about her in vain his whitest snows; and now the woods were turning green.

It was merely in keeping with Gabriella's nature, therefore, that as she grew to know the people among whom she had come to stay, their homes, their family histories, one household and one story should have engaged her deep interest: David's parents and David's career. As she drove about the country, visiting with the farmer's wife, there had been pointed out a melancholy remnant of a farm, desperately resisting absorption by some one of three growing estates touching it on three sides. She had been taken to call on the father and mother; had seen the poverty within doors, the half-ruined condition of the outhouses; had heard of their son, now away at the university; of how they had saved and he had struggled. A proud father it was who now told of his son's magnificent progress already at college.

"Ah," she exclaimed, thinking it over in her room that night, "this is something worth hearing! Here is the hero in life! Among these easy-going people this solitary struggler. I, too, am one now; I can understand him."

During the first year of her teaching, there had

developed in her a noble desire to see David; but one long to be disappointed. He did not return home during his vacation; she went away during hers. The autumn following he was back in college; she at her school. Then the Christmas holidays and his astounding, terrible home-coming, put out of college and church. As soon as she heard of that awful downfall, Gabriella felt a desire to go straight to him. She did not reason or hesitate: she went.

And now for two months they had been seeing each other every few days.

Thus by the working out of vast forces, the lives of Gabriella and David had been jostled violently together. They were the children of two revolutions, separate yet having a common end: she produced by the social revolution of the New World, which overthrew mediaeval slavery; he by the intellectual revolution of the Old World, which began to put forth scientific law, but in doing this brought on one of the greatest ages of religious doubt. So that both were early vestiges of the same immeasurable race evolution, proceeding along converging lines. She, living on the artificial summits of a decaying social order, had farthest to fall, in its collapse, ere she reached the natural earth; he, toiling at the bottom, had farthest to rise before he could look out upon the plains of widening modern thought and man's evolving destiny. Through her fall and his rise, they had been brought to a common level. But on that level all that had befallen her had driven her as out of a blinding storm into the church, the seat and asylum of religion; all that had befallen him had driven him out of the churches as the fortifications of theology. She had been drawn to that part of worship which lasts and is divine;

he had been repelled by the part that passes and is human.

XVI

Although Gabriella had joyously greeted the day, as bringing exemption from stifling hours in school, her spirits had drooped ere evening with monotony. There were no books in use among the members of that lovable household except school-books; they were too busy with the primary joys of life to notice the secondary resources of literature. She had no pleasant sewing. To escape the noise of the pent-up children, she must restrict herself to that part of the house which comprised her room. A walk out of doors was impracticable, although she ventured once into the yard to study more closely the marvels of the ice-work; and to the edge of the orchard, to ascertain how the apple trees were bearing up under those avalanches of frozen silver slipped from the clouds.

So there were empty hours for her that day; and always the emptiest are the heaviest - those unfilled baskets of time which strangely become lightest only after we have heaped them with the best we have to give. Gabriella filled the hour-baskets this day with thoughts of David, whose field work she knew would be interrupted by the storm, and whose movements about the house she vainly tried to follow in imagination.

Two months of close association with him in that dull country neighborhood had wrought great changes in the simple feeling with which she had sought him at first. He had then been to her only a Prodigal who had squandered his substance, tried to feed his soul on the swinish husks of Doubt, and returning to his father's house unrepentant, had been admitted yet remained rejected: a Prodigal not of the flesh and the world but of the spirit and the Lord. But what has ever interested the heart of woman as a prodigal of some kind?

At other times he was figured by her sympathies as a young Samaritan gone travelling into a Divine country but fallen among spiritual thieves, who had stripped him of his seamless robe of Faith and left him bruised by Life's wayside: a maltreated Christ-neighbor whom it was her duty to succor if she could. But a woman's nursing of a man's wound - how often it becomes the nursing of the wounded! Moreover, Gabriella had now long been aware of what she had become to her prodigal, her Samaritan; she saw the truth and watched it growing from day to day; for he was incapable of disguises. But often what effect has such watching upon the watcher, a watcher who is alone in the world? So that while she fathomed with many feminine soundings all that she was to David, Gabriella did not dream what David had become to her.

Shortly after nightfall, when she heard his heavy tread on the porch below, the tedium of the day instantly vanished. Happiness rose in her like a clear fountain set suddenly playing - rose to her eyes - bathed her in refreshing vital emotions.

"I am so glad you came," she said as she entered the parlor, gave him her hand, and stood looking up into his softened rugged face, at his majestical head, which overawed her a little always. Large as was the mould in which nature had cast his body, this seemed to her dwarfed by the inner largeness of the man, whose development she could note as now going forward almost visibly from day to day: he had risen so far already and was still so young.

He did not reply to her greeting except with a look. In matters which involved his feeling for her, he was habitually hampered and ill at ease; only on general subjects did she ever see him master of his resources. Gabriella had fallen into the habit of looking into his eyes for the best answers: there he always spoke not only with ideas but emotions: a double speech much cared for by woman.

They seated themselves on opposite sides of the wide deep fire-place: a grate for soft coal had not yet destroyed that.

"Your schoolhouse is safe," he announced briefly.

"Oh, I've been wanting to know all day but had no one to send! How do YOU know?" she inquired quickly.

"It's safe. The yard will have to be cleared of brush: that's all."

She looked at him gratefully. "You are always so kind!"

"Well," observed David, with a great forward stride, "aren't you?"

Gabriella, being a woman, did not particularly prize this remark: it suggested his being kind because she had been kind; and a woman likes nothing as reward, everything as tribute.

"And now if the apple trees are only not killed!" she exclaimed joyously, changing the subject.

"Why the apple trees?"

"If you had been here last spring, you would have understood. When they bloom, they are mine, I take possession." After a moment she added: "They bring back the recollection of such happy times - springs long ago. Some time I'll tell you."

"When you were a little girl?"

"Yes."

"I wish I had known you when you were a little girl," said David, in an undertone, looking into the fire.

Gabriella reflected how impossible this would have been: the thought caused her sharp pain.

Some time later, David, who had appeared more and more involved in some inward struggle, suddenly asked a relieving question: -

"Do you know the first time I ever saw you?"

She did not answer at once.

"In the smoke-house," she said with a ripple of laughter. Gabriella, when she was merry, made one, think of some lovely green April hill, snow-capped.

David shook his head slowly. His eyes grew soft

and mysterious.

"It was the first time *I* ever saw YOU," she protested.

He continued to shake his head, and she looked puzzled.

"You saw me once before that, and smiled at me."

Gabriella seemed incredulous and not well pleased.

After a little while David began in the manner of one who sets out to tell a story he is secretly fond of.

"Do you remember standing on the steps of a church the Friday evening before Christmas - a little after dark?"

Gabriella's eyes began to express remembrance. "A wagon-load of cedar had just been thrown out on the sidewalk, the sexton was carrying it into the church, some children were helping, you were making a wreath: do you remember?"

She knew every word of this.

"A young man - a Bible student - passed, or tried to pass. You smiled at his difficulty. Not unkindly," he added, smiling not unkindly himself.

"And that was you? This explains why I have always believed I had seen you before. But it was only for a moment, your face was in the dark; how should I remember?"

After she said this, she looked grave: his face that night

had been far from a happy one.

"That day," continued David, quickly grave also, "that day I saw my professors and pastor for the last time; it ended me as a Bible student. I had left the University and the scene of my trial only a little while before."

He rose as he concluded and took a turn across the room. Then he faced her, smiling a little sadly.

"Once I might have thought all that Providential. I mean, seeing the faces of my professors - my judges - last, as the end of my old life; then seeing your face next - the beginning of the new."

He had long used frankness like this, making no secret of himself, of her influence over him. It was embarrassing; it declared so much, assumed so much, that had never been declared or assumed in any other way. But her stripped and beaten young Samaritan was no labyrinthine courtier, bescented and bedraped and bedyed with worldliness and conventions: he came ever in her presence naked of soul. It was this that empowered her to take the measure of his feeling for her: it had its effect.

David returned to his chair and looked across with a mixture of hesitancy and determination.

"I have never spoken to you about my expulsion - my unbelief."

After a painful pause she answered.

"You must be aware that I have noticed your silence. Perhaps you do not realize how much I have regretted it."

"You know why I have not?"

She did not answer.

"I have been afraid. It's the only thing in the world I've ever been afraid of."

"Why should you have been?"

"I dreaded to know how you might feel. It has caused a difficulty with every one so far. It separated me from my friends among the Bible students. It separated me from my professors, my pastor. It has alienated my father and mother. I did not know how you would regard it."

"Have I not known it all the time? Has it made any difference?"

"Ah! but that might be only your toleration! Meantime it has become a question with me how far your toleration will go - what is back of your toleration! We tolerate so much in people who are merely acquaintances - people that we do not care particularly for and that we are never to have anything to do with in life. But if the tie begins to be closer, then the things we tolerated at a distance - what becomes of them then? "

He was looking at her steadily, and she dropped her eyes. This was another one of the Prodigal's assumptions - but never before put so pointedly.

"So I have feared that when I myself told you what I

believe and what I do not believe, it might be the end of me. And when you learned my feelings toward what YOU believe - that might be more troublesome still. But the time has come when I must know."

He turned his face away from her, and rising, walked several times across the room.

At last also the moment had arrived for which she had been waiting. Freely as they had spoken to each other of their pasts - she giving him glimpses of the world in which she had been reared, he taking her into his world which was equally unfamiliar - on this subject silence between them had never been broken. She had often sought to pass the guard he placed around this tragical episode but had always been turned away. The only original ground of her interest in him, therefore, still remained a background, obscure and unexplored. She regretted this for many reasons. Her belief was that he was merely passing through a phase of religious life not uncommon with those who were born to go far in mental travels before they settled in their Holy Land. She believed it would be over the sooner if he had the chance to live it out in discussion; and she herself offered the only possibility of this. Gabriella was in a position to know by experience what it means in hours of trouble to need the relief of companionship. Ideas, she had learned, long shut up in the mind tend to germinate and take root. There had been discords which had ceased sounding in her own ear as soon as they were poured into another.

"I have always hoped," she repeated, as he seated himself, "that you would talk with me about these things." And then to divert the conversation into less difficult channels, she added: -

"As to what you may think of my beliefs, I have no fear; they need not be discussed and they cannot be attacked."

"You are an Episcopalian," he suggested hesitatingly. "I do not wish to be rude, but - your church has its dogmas."

"There is not a dogma of my church that I have ever thought of for a moment: or of any other church," she replied instantly and clearly.

In those simple words she had uttered unaware a long historic truth: that religion, not theology, forms the spiritual life of women. In the whole history of the world's opinions, no dogma of any weight has ever originated with a woman; wherein, as in many other ways, she shows points of superiority in her intellect. It is a man who tries to apprehend God through his logic and psychology; a woman understands Him better through emotions and deeds. It is the men who are concerned about the cubits, the cedar wood, the Urim and Thummim of the Tabernacle; woman walks straight into the Holy of Holies. Men constructed the Cross; women wept for the Crucified. It was a man - a Jew defending his faith in his own supernatural revelation - who tried to ram a sponge of vinegar into the mouth of Christ, dying; it was women who gathered at the sepulchre of Resurrection. If Christ could have had a few women among his Apostles, there might have been more of His religion in the world and fewer creeds barnacled on the World's Ship of Souls.

"How can you remain in your church without either believing or disbelieving its dogmas ? " asked

David, squarely.

"My church is the altar of Christ and the house of God," replied Gabriella, simply. "And so is any other church." That was all the logic she had and all the faith she needed; beyond that limit she did not even think.

"And you believe in THEM ALL?" he asked with wondering admiration.

"I believe in them all."

"Once I did also," observed David, reverently and with new reverence for her.

"What I regret is that you should have thrown away your religion on account of your difficulties with theology. Nothing more awful could have befallen you than that."

"It was the churches that made the difficulties," said David, "I did not. But there is more than theology in it. You do not know what I think about religions - revelations - inspirations - man's place in nature."

"What DO you think?" she asked eagerly. "I suppose now I shall hear something about those great books."

She put herself at ease in her chair like one who prepares to listen quietly.

"Shall I tell you how the whole argument runs as I have arranged it? I shall have to begin far away and come down to the subject by degrees." He looked apologetic.

"Tell me everything; I have been waiting a long time."

David reflected a few moments and then began: -

"The first of my books as I have arranged them, considers what we call the physical universe as a whole - our heavens - the stars - and discusses the little that man knows about it. I used to think the earth was the centre of this universe, the most important world in it, on account of Man. That is what the ancient Hebrews thought. In this room float millions of dust-particles too small to be seen by us. To say that the universe is made for the sake of the earth would be something like saying that the earth was created for the sake of one of these particles of its own dust."

He paused to see how she received this.

"That ought to be a great book," she said approvingly. "I should like to study it."

"The second takes up that small part of the universe which we call our solar system and sums up the little we have learned regarding it. I used to think the earth the most important part of the solar system, on account of Man. So the earliest natural philosophers believed. That is like believing that the American continent was created for the sake, say, of my father's farm."

He awaited her comment.

"That should be a great book," she said simply. "Some day let me see THAT."

"The third detaches for study one small planet of that system - our earth - and reviews our latest knowledge of that: as to how it has been evolved into its present stage of existence through other stages requiring unknown millions and millions and millions of years. Once I thought it was created in six days. So it is written. Do you believe that? "

There was silence.

"What is the next book?" she asked.

"The fourth," said David, with a twinkle in his eye at her refusal to answer his question, "takes up the history of the earth's surface - its crust - the layers of this - as one might study the skin of an apple as large as the globe. In the course of an almost infinite time, as we measure things, it discovers the appearance of Life on this crust, and then tries to follow the progress of Life from the lowest forms upward, always upward, to Man: another time infinitely vast, according to our standards."

He looked over for some comment but she made none, and he continued, his interest deepening, his face kindling: -

"The fifth takes up the subject of Man, as a single one of the myriads of forms of Life that have grown on the earth's crust, and gives the best of what we know of him viewed as a species of animal. Does this tire you? "

Gabriella made the only gesture of displeasure he had ever seen.

"Now," said David, straightening himself up, "I draw near to the root of the matter. A sixth book takes up what we call the civilization of this animal species, Man. It subdivides his civilization into different civilizations. It analyzes these civilizations, where it is possible, into their arts, governments, literatures, religions, and other elements. And the seventh," he resumed after a grave pause, scrutinizing her face most eagerly, "the seventh takes up just one part of his civilizations - the religions of the globe - and gives an account of these. It describes how they have grown and flourished, how some have passed as absolutely away as the civilizations that produced them. It teaches that those religions were as natural a part of those civilizations as their civil laws, their games, their wars, their philosophy; that the religious books of these races, which they themselves often thought inspired revelations, were no more inspired and no more revelations than their secular books; that Buddha's faith or Brahma's were no more direct from God than Buddhistic or Brahman temples were from God; that the Koran is no more inspired than Moorish architecture is inspired; that the ancient religion of the Jewish race stands on the same footing as the other great religions of the globe - as to being Supernatural; that the second religion of the Hebrews, starting out of them, but rejected by them, the Christian religion, the greatest of all to us, takes its place with the others as a perfectly natural expression of the same human desire and effort to find God and to worship Him through all the best that we know in ourselves and of the universe outside us."

"Ah," said Gabriella, suddenly leaning forward in her chair, "that is the book that has done all the harm."

"One moment! All these books," continued David, for he was aroused now and did not pause to consider her passionate protest, "have this in common: that they try to discover and to trace Law. The universe - it is the expression of Law. Our solar system - it has been formed by Law, The sun - the driving force of Law has made it. Our earth - Law has shaped that; brought Life out of it; evolved Life on it from the lowest to the highest; lifted primeval Man to modern Man; out of barbarism developed civilization; out of prehistoric religions, historic religions. And this one order - method - purpose - ever running and unfolding through the universe, is all that we know of Him whom we call Creator, God, our Father. So that His reign is the Reign of Law. He, Himself, is the author of the Law that we should seek Him. We obey, and our seekings are our religions."

"If you ask me whether I believe in the God of the Hebrews, I say 'Yes'; just as I believe in the God of the Babylonians, of the Egyptians, of the Greeks, of the Romans, of all men. But if you ask whether I believe what the Hebrews wrote of God, or what any other age or people thought of God, I say ' No.' I believe what the best thought of my own age thinks of Him in the light of man's whole past and of our greater present knowledge of the Laws of His universe," said David, stoutly, speaking for his masters.

"As for the theologies," he resumed hastily, as if not wishing to be interrupted, "I know of no book that has undertaken to number them. They, too, are part of Man's nature and civilization, of his never ceasing search. But they are merely what he thinks of God - never anything more. They often contain the highest thought of which he is capable in his time and place; but the awful mistake and cruelty of them is that they have regularly been put forth as the voice of God

Himself, authoritative, inviolable, and unchanging. An assemblage of men have a perfect right to turn a man out of their church on theological grounds; but they have no right to do it in the name of God. With as much propriety a man might be expelled from a political party in the name of God. In the long life of any one of the great religions of the globe, how many brief theologies have grown up under it like annual plants under a tree! How many has the Christian religion itself sprouted, nourished, and trampled down as dead weeds! What do we think now of the Christian theology of the tenth century? of the twelfth? of the fifteenth? In the nineteenth century alone, how many systems of theology have there been? In the Protestantism of the United States, how many are there to-day? Think of the names they bear - older and newer! According to founders, and places, and sources, and contents, and methods: Arminian - Augustinian - Calvinistic - Lutheran - Gallican - Genevan - Mercersburg - New England - Oxford - national - revealed - Catholic - evangelical - fundamental - historical - homiletical - moral - mystical - pastoral - practical - dogmatic - exegetical - polemic - rational - systematic. That sounds a little like Polonius," said David, stopping suddenly, "but there is no humor in it! One great lesson in the history of them all is not to be neglected: that through them also runs the great Law of Evolution, of the widening thoughts of men; so that now, in civilized countries at least, the churches persecute to the death no longer. You know what the Egyptian Priesthood would have done with me at my trial. What the Mediaeval hierarchy would have done. What the Protestant or the Catholic theology of two centuries ago might have done. Now mankind is developing better ideas of these little arrangements of human psychology on the subject of God, though the churches still try to enforce them in His name. But the time is coming when the churches will be deserted by all thinking men, unless they cease trying to uphold, as the teachings of God, mere creeds of their ecclesiastical founders. Very few men reject all belief in God; and it is no man's right to inquire in what any man's belief consists; men do reject and have a right to reject what some man writes out as the eternal truth of the matter."

"And now," he said, turning to her sorrowfully, "that is the best or the worst of what I believe - according as one may like it or not like it. I see all things as a growth, a sublime unfolding by the Laws of God. The race ever rises toward Him. The old things which were its best once die off from it as no longer good. Its charity grows, its justice grows. All the nobler, finer elements of its spirit come forth more and more - a continuous advance along the paths of Law. And the better the world, the larger its knowledge, the easier its faith in Him who made it and who leads it on. The development of Man is itself the great Revelation of Him! But I have studied these things ignorantly, only a little while. I am at the beginning of my life, and hope to grow. Still I stand where I have placed myself. And now, are you like the others: do you give me up?"

He faced her with the manner in which he had sat before his professors, conceiving himself as on trial a second time. He had in him the stuff of martyrs and was prepared to stand by his faith at the cost of all things.

The silence in the room lasted. Her feeling for him was so much deeper than all this - so centred, not in what his faith was to her but in what HE was to her, that she did not trust herself to speak. He was not on trial in these matters in the least: without his knowing it, he had been on trial in many other ways for a long time.

He misunderstood her silence, read wrongly her expression which was obeying with some severity the need she felt to conceal what she had no right to show.

"Ah, well! Ah, well!" he cried piteously, rising slowly.

When she saw his face a moment later across the room as he turned, it was the face she had first seen in the dark street. It had stopped her singing then; it drew an immediate response from her now. She crossed over to him and took one of his hands in both of hers. Her cheeks were flushed, her voice trembled.

"I am not your judge," she said, "and in all this there is only one thing that is too sad, too awful, for me to accept. I am sorry you should have been misled into believing that the Christian religion is nothing more than one of the religions of the world, and Christ merely one of its religious teachers. I wish with all my strength you believed as you once believed, that the Bible is a direct Revelation from God, making known to us, beyond all doubt, the Resurrection of the dead, the Immortality of the Soul, in a better world than this, and the presence with us of a Father who knows our wants, pities our weakness, and answers our prayers. But I believe you will one day regain your faith: you will come back to the Church."

He shook his head.

"Don't be deceived," he said.

"Men, great men, have said that before and they have come back. I am a woman, and these questions never trouble us; but is it not a common occurrence that men who think deeply on such mysteries pass through their period of doubt?"

"But suppose I never pass through mine! You have not answered my question," he said determinedly. "Does this make no difference in your feeling for me? Would it make none?"

"Will you bring me that book on the religions of the world?"

"Ah," he said, "you have not answered."

"I have told you that I am not your judge."

"Ah, but that tells nothing: a woman is never a judge. She is either with one or against him."

"Which do I look like?" - she laughed evasively - "Mercy or Vengeance? And have you forgotten that it is late - too late to ask questions?"

He stood, comprehending her doubtfully, with immeasurable joy, and then went out to get his overcoat.

"Bring your things in here," she said, "it is cold in the hall. And wrap up warmly! That is more important than all the Genevan and the homiletical!"

He bade her good night, subdued with happiness that seemed to blot out the troublous past, to be the beginning of new life. New happiness brought new awkwardness: -

"This was not my regular night," he said threateningly. "I came to-night instead of to-morrow night."

Gabriella could answer a remark like that quickly enough.

"Certainly: it is hard to wait even for a slight pleasure, and it is best to be through with suffering."

He looked as if cold water and hot water had been thrown on him at the same time: he received shocks of different kinds and was doubtful as to the result. He shook his head questioningly.

"I may do very well with science, but I am not so sure about women."

"Aren't women science?"

"They are a branch of theology," he said; "they are what a man thinks about when he begins to probe his Destiny!"

XVII

David slept peacefully that night, like a man who has reached the end of long suspense. When he threw his shutters open late, he found that the storm had finished its work and gone and that the weather had settled stinging cold. The heavens were hyacinth, the ground white with snow; and the sun, day-lamp of that vast ceiling of blue, made the earth radiant as for the bridal morn of Winter. So HIS thoughts ran.

"Gabriella! Gabriella!" he cried, as he beheld the beauty, the purity, the breadth, the clearness. "It is you - except the coldness, the cruelty."

All day then those three: the hyacinthine sky, the flashing lamp, the white earth, with not one crystal thawing.

It being Saturday, there was double work for him. He knocked up the wood for that day and for Sunday also, packed and stored it; cut double the quantity of oats; threw over twice the usual amount of fodder. The shocks were buried. He had hard kicking to do before he reached the rich brown fragrant stalks. Afterwards he made paths through the snow about the house for his mother; to the dairy, to the hen-house. In the wooden monotony of her life an interruption in these customary visits would have been to her a great loss.

The snow being over the cook's shoe-tops, he took a basket and dug the vegetables out of the holes in the garden.

In the afternoon he had gone to the pond in the woods to cut a drinking place for the cattle. As he was returning with his axe on his shoulder, the water on it having instantly frozen, he saw riding away across the stable lot, the one of their neighbors who was causing him so much trouble about the buying of the farm. He stopped hot with anger and watched him.

In those years a westward movement was taking place among the Kentuckians - a sad exodus. Many families rendered insolvent or bankrupt by the war and the loss of their slaves, while others interspersed among them had grown richer by Government contracts, were now being bought out, forced out, by debt or mortgage, and were seeking new homes where lay cheaper lands and escape from the suffering of living on, ruined, amid old prosperous acquaintances. It was a profound historic disturbance of population, destined later on to affect profoundly many younger commonwealths. This was the situation now bearing heavily on David's father, on three sides of whose fragmentary estate lay rich neighbors, one of whom especially desired it.

The young man threw his axe over his shoulder again and took a line straight toward the house.

"He shall not take advantage of my father's weakness again," he said, "nor shall he use to further his purposes what I have done to reduce him to this want."

He felt sure that this pressure upon his father lay in part back of the feeling of his parents toward him. His expulsion from college and their belief that he was a failure; the fact that for three years repairs had been neglected and improvements allowed to wait, in order that all possible revenues might be collected for him; even these caused them less acute distress than the fear that as a consequence they should now be forced so late in life to make that mournful pilgrimage into strange regions. David was saddened to think that ever at his father's side sat his mother, irritating him by dropping all day into his ear the half idle, half intentional words which are the water that wears out the rock.

The young man walked in a straight line toward the house, determined to ascertain the reason of this last visit, and to have out the long-awaited talk with his father. He reached the yard gate, then paused and wheeled abruptly toward the barn.

"Not to-day," he said, thinking of Gabriella and of his coming visit to her now but a few hours off. "To-morrow! Day after to-morrow! Any time after this! But no quarrels to-day!" and his face softened.

Before the barn door, where the snow had been tramped down by the stock and seeds of grain lay scattered, he flushed a flock of little birds, nearly all strangers to each other. Some from the trees about the yard; some from the thickets, fences, and fields farther away. As he threw open the barn doors, a few more, shyer still, darted swiftly into hiding. He heard the quick heavy flap of wings on the joists of the oats loft overhead, and a hawk swooped out the back door and sailed low away.

The barn had become a battle-field of hunger and life.

This was the second day of famine - all seeds being buried first under ice and now under snow; swift hunger sending the littler ones to this granary, the larger following to prey on them. To-night there would be owls and in the darkness tragedies. In the morning, perhaps, he would find a feather which had floated from a breast. A hundred years ago, he reflected, the wolves would have gathered here also and the cougar and the wildcat for bigger game.

It was sunset as he left the stable, his work done. Beside the yard gate there stood a locust tree, and on a bough of this, midway up, for he never goes to the tree-tops at this season, David saw a cardinal. He was sitting with his breast toward the clear crimson sky; every twig around him silver filigree; the whole tree glittering with a million gems of rose and white, gold and green; and wherever a fork, there a hanging of snow. The bird's crest was shot up. He had come forth to look abroad upon this strange wreck of nature and peril to his kind. David had scarcely stopped before him when with a quick shy movement he dived down into one of his ruined winter fortresses-a cedar dismembered and flattened out, never to rise again.

The supper that evening was a very quiet one. David felt that his father's eyes were often on him reproachfully; and that his mother's were approvingly on his father's. Time and again during the meal the impulse well-nigh overcame him to speak to his father then and there; but he knew it would be a cruel, angry scene; and each time the face of Gabriella restrained him. It was for peace; and his heart shut out all discord from around that new tenderer figure of her which had come forth within him this day.

Soon even the trouble at home was forgotten; he was on his way through the deep snow toward her.

XVIII

Gabriella had brought with her into this neighborhood of good-natured, non-reading people the recollections of literature. These became her library of the mind; and deep joy she drew from its invisible volumes. She had transported a fine collection of the heroes and heroines of good fiction (Gabriella, according to the usage of her class and time, had never read any but standard works). These, when the earlier years of adversity came on, had been her second refuge from the world:, religion was the first. Now they were the means by which she returned to the world in imagination. The failure to gather together so durable a company of friends leaves every mind the more destitute - especially a woman's, which has greater need to live upon ideals, and cannot always find these in actual life. Then there were short poems and parts of long poems, which were as texts out of a high and beautiful Gospel of Nature. One of these was on the snowstorm; and this same morning her memory long was busy, fitting the poem within her mind to the scenery around the farmhouse, as she passed joyously from window to window, looking out far and near.

There it all was as the great New England poet had described it: that masonry out of an unseen quarry, that frolic architecture of the snow, nightwork of the North Wind, fierce artificer. In a few hours he had mimicked with wild and savage fancy the structures which human art can scarce rear, stone by stone, in an age: white bastions curved with projected roof round every windward stake or tree or door; the gateway over-topped with tapering turrets; coop and kennel hung mockingly with Parian wreaths; a swanlike form investing the hidden thorn.

From one upper window under the blue sky in the distance she could see what the poet had never beheld: a field of hemp shocks looking like a winter camp, dazzlingly white. The scene brought to her mind some verses written by a minor Kentucky writer on his own soil and people.

SONG OF THE HEMP

Ah, gentle are the days when the Year is young
And rolling fields with rippling hemp are green
And from old orchards pipes the thrush at morn.
No land, no land like this is yet unsung
Where man and maid at twilight meet unseen
And Love is born.

Oh, mighty summer days and god of flaming tress
When in the fields full-headed bends the stalk,
And blossoms what was sown!
No land, no land like this for tenderness
When man and maid as one together walk
And Love is grown.

Oh, dim, dim autumn days of sobbing rain
When on the fields the ripened hemp is spread
And woods are brown.
No land, no land like this for mortal pain
When Love stands weeping by the sweet, sweet bed

James Lane Allen

For Love cut down.

Ah, dark, unfathomably dark, white winter days
When falls the sun from out the crystal deep
On muffled farms.
No land, no land like this for God's sad ways
When near the tented fields Love's Soldier lies asleep
With empty arms.

The verses were too sorrowful for this day, with its
new, half-awakened happiness. Had Gabriella been
some strong-minded, uncompromising New England
woman, she might have ended her association with
David the night before - taking her place triumphantly
beside an Accusing Judge. Or she might all the more
fiercely have set on him an acrid conscience, and
begun battling with him through the evidences of
Christianity, that she might save his soul. But this was
a Southern girl of strong, warm, deep nature, who felt
David's life in its simple entirety, and had no thought
of rejecting the whole on account of some peculiarity
in one of its parts; the white flock was more to her than
one dark member. Inexpressibly dear and sacred as
was her own church, her own faith, she had never been
taught to estimate a man primarily with reference to
his. What was his family, how he stood in his
profession, his honorable character, his manners, his
manhood - these were what Gabriella had always been
taught to look for first in a man.

In many other ways than in his faith and doubt David
was a new type of man to her. He was the most
religious, the only religious, one she had ever known -
a new spiritual growth arising out of his people as a
young oak out of the soil. Had she been familiar with
the Greek idea, she might have called him a Kentucky

autochthon. It was the first time also that she had ever encountered in a Kentuckian the type of student mind - that fitness and taste for scholarship which sometimes moves so unobtrusively and rises so high among that people, but is usually unobserved unless discovered pre-eminent and commanding far from the confines of the state.

Touching his scepticism she looked upon him still as she had thought of him at first, - as an example of a sincere soul led astray for a time only. Strange as were his views (and far stranger they seemed in those years than now), she felt no doubt that when the clouds marshalled across his clear vision from the minds of others had been withdrawn, he would once more behold the Sun of Righteousness as she did. Gabriella as by intuition reasoned that a good life most often leads to a belief in the Divine Goodness; that as we understand in others only what we are in ourselves, so it is the highest elements of humanity that must be relied upon to believe in the Most High: and of David's lofty nature she possessed the whole history of his life as evidence.

Her last act, then, the night before had been, in her nightgown, on her knees, to offer up a prayer that he might be saved from the influences of false teachers and guided back to the only Great One. But when a girl, with all the feelings which belong to her at that hour, seeks this pure audience and sends upward the name of a man on her spotless prayers, he is already a sacred happiness to her as well as a care.

On this day she was radiant with tender happiness. The snow of itself was exhilarating. It spread around her an enchanted land. It buried out of sight in the yard and stable lots all mire, all ugly things. This ennoblement of eternal objects reacted with comic effect on the interior of the house itself; outside it was a marble palace, surrounded by statuary; within - alas! It provoked her humor, that innocent fun-making which many a time had rendered her environment the more tolerable.

When she went down into the parlor early that evening to await David's coming, this gayety, this laughter of the generations of men and women who made up her past, possessed her still. She made a fresh investigation of the parlor, took a new estimate of its peculiar furnishings. The hearthstones - lead color. The mohair furniture - cold at all temperatures of the room and slippery in every position of the body. The little marble-top table on which rested a glass case holding a stuffed blue jay clutching a varnished limb: tail and eyes stretched beyond the reach of muscles. Near the door an enormous shell which, on summer days, the cook blew as a dinner horn for the hands in the field. A collection of ambrotypes which, no matter how held, always caused the sitter to look as though the sun was shining in his eyes. The violence of the Brussels carpet. But the cheap family portraits in thin wooden frames - these were Gabriella's delight in a mood like this.

The first time she saw these portraits, she turned and walked rapidly out of the parlor. She had enough troubles of her own without bearing the troubles of all these faces. Later on she could confront them with equanimity - that company of the pallid, the desperately sick, the unaccountably uncomfortable. All looked, not as though there had been a death in the family, but a death in the collection: only the same grief could have so united them as mourners. And whatever else they lacked, each showed two hands, the full number, placed where they were sure to be counted.

She was in the midst of this psychological reversion to ancestral gayety when David arrived. Each looked quickly at the other with unconscious fear. Within a night and a day each had drawn nearer to the other; and each secretly inquired whether the other now discovered this nearness. Gabriella saw at least that he, too, was excited with happiness.

He appeared to her for the first time handsome. He WAS better looking. When one approaches the confines of love, one nears the borders of beauty. Nature sets going a certain work of decoration, of transformation. Had David about this time been a grouse, he would probably have displayed a prodigious ruff. Had he been a bulbul and continued to feel as he did, he would have poured into the ear of night such roundelays as had never been conceived of by that disciplined singer. Had he been a master violinist, he would have been unable to play a note from a wild desire to flourish the bow. He had long stood rooted passively in the soil of being like a century plant when it is merely keeping itself in existence. But latterly, feeling in advance the approach of the Great Blossoming Hour, he had begun to shoot up rapidly into a lofty life-stalk; there were inches of the rankest growth on him within the last twenty-four hours. To-night he was not even serious in his conversation; and therefore he was the more awkward. His emotions were unmanageable; much more his talk. But she who witnesses this awkwardness and understands - does she ever fail to pardon?

"Last night," he said with a droll twinkle, after the evening was about half spent, "there was one subject I did not speak to you about - Man's place in Nature. Have you ever thought about that?"

"I've been too busy thinking about my place in the school!" said Gabriella, laughing - Gabriella who at all times was simplicity and clearness.

"You see Nature does nothing for Man except what she enables him to do for himself. In this way she has made a man of him; she has given him his resources and then thrown him upon them. Beyond that she cares nothing, does nothing, provides, arranges nothing. I used to think, for instance, that the greenness of the earth was intended for his eyes - all the loveliness of spring. On the contrary, she merely gave him an eye which has adapted itself to get pleasure out of the greenness. The beauty of spring would have been the same, year after year, century after century, had he never existed. And the blue of the sky - I used to think it was hung about the earth for his sake; and the colors of the clouds, the great sunsets. But the blueness of the sky is nothing but the dust of the planet floating deep around it, too light to sink through the atmosphere, but reflecting the rays of the sun. These rays fall on the clouds and color them. It would all have been so, had Man never been born. The earth's springs of drinking water, refreshing showers, the rainbow on the cloud, - they would have been the same, had no human being ever stood on this planet to claim them for ages as the signs of providence and of covenant."

Gabriella had her own faith as to the rainbow.

"So , none of the other animals was made for Man,"

resumed David, who seemed to have some ulterior purpose in all this. "I used to think the structure and nature of the ass were given him that he might be adapted to bear Man's burdens; they were given him that he might bear his own burdens. Horses were not made for cavalry. And a camel - I never doubted that he was a wonderful contrivance to enable man to cross the desert; he is a wonderful contrivance in order that the contrivance itself may cross the desert."

"I hope I may never have to use one," said Gabriella, "when I commence to ride again. I prefer horses and carriages - though I suppose you would say that only the carriage was designed for me and that I had no right to be drawn in that way."

"Some day a horse may be designed for you, just as the carriage is. We do not use horses on railroads now; we did use them at first in Kentucky. Sometime you may not use horses in your carriage. You may have a horse that was designed for you."

"I think," said Gabriella, "I should prefer a horse that was designed for itself."

"And so," resumed David, moving straight on toward his concealed climax, "if I were a poet, I'd never write poems about flowers and clouds and lakes and mountains and moonbeams and all that; those things are not for a man. If I were a novelist, I'd never write stories about a grizzly bear, or a dog, or a red bird. If I were a sculptor, I'd not carve a lynx or a lion. If I were a painter, I'd never paint sheep. In all this universe there is only one thing that Nature ever created for a man. I'd write poems about that one thing! I'd write novels about it! I'd paint it! I'd carve it! I'd compose music to it!"

"Why, what is that?" said Gabriella, led sadly astray.

"A woman!" said David solemnly, turning red.

Gabriella fled into the uttermost caves of silence.

"And there was only one thing ever made for woman."

"I understand perfectly."

David felt rebuffed. He hardly knew why. But after a moment or two of silence he went on, still advancing with rough paces toward his goal: -

"Sometimes," he said mournfully, "it's harder for a man to get the only thing in the world that was ever made for him than anything else! This difficulty, however, appertains exclusively to the human species."

Gabriella touched her handkerchief quickly to her lips and held it there.

"But then, many curious things are true of our species," he continued, with his eyes on the fire and in the manner of a soliloquy, "that never occur elsewhere. A man, for instance, is the only animal that will settle comfortably down for the rest of its days to live on the exertions of the female."

"It shows how a woman likes to be depended on," said Gabriella, with her deep womanliness.

"Tom-cats of the fireside," said David, "who are proud of what fat mice their wives feed them on. It may show what you say in the nature of the woman. But what does it show in the nature of the man?"

"That depends."

"I don't think it depends," replied David. "I think it is either one of the results of Christianity or a survival of barbarism. As one of the results of Christianity, it demonstrates what women will endure when they are imposed upon. As a relic of barbarism - when it happens in our country - why not regard it as derived from the North American Indians? The chiefs lounged around the house and smoked the best tobacco and sent the squaws out to work for them. Occasionally they broke silence by briefly declaring that they thought themselves immortal."

Gabriella tried to draw the conversation into other channels, but David was not to be diverted.

"It has been a great fact in the history of your sex," he said, looking across at her, with a shake of his head, as though she did not appreciate the subject, "that idea that everything in the universe was made for Man."

"Why?" inquired Gabriella, resigning herself to the perilous and the irresistible.

"Well, in old times it led men to think that since everything else belonged to them, so did woman: therefore when they wanted her they did not ask for her; they took her."

"It is much better arranged at present, whatever the reason."

"Now a man cannot always get one, even when he asks for her," and David turned red again and knotted his hands.

"I am so glad the schoolhouse was not damaged by the storm," observed Gabriella, reflecting.

David fell into a revery but presently awoke.

"There are more men than women in the world. On an average, that is only a fraction of a woman to every man. Still the men cannot take care of them. But it ought to be a real pleasure to every man to take care of an entire woman."

"Did you ever notice the hands in that portrait?"

David glanced at the portrait without noticing it, and went his way.

"Since a man knows nothing else was created for him, he feels his loneliness without her so much more deeply. They ought to be very good and true to each other - a man and a woman - since they two are alone in the universe."

He gulped down his words and stood up, trembling.

"I must be going," he said, without even looking at Gabriella, and went out into the hall for his coat.

"Bring it in here." she called. "It is cold out there." She watched how careless he was about making himself snug for his benumbing walk. He had a woollen comforter which he left loosely tied about his neck.

"Tie it closer," she commanded. "You had a cold last night, and it is worse tonight. Tuck it in close about your neck."

David made the attempt. He was not thinking.

"This way!" And Gabriella showed him by using her fingers around her own neck and collar.

He tried again and failed, standing before her with a mingling of embarrassment and stubborn determination.

"That will never do!" she cried with genuine concern. She took hold of the comforter by the ends and drew the knot up close to his throat, he lifting his head to receive it as it came. Then David with his eyes on the ceiling felt his coat collar turned up and her soft warm fingers tucking the comforter in around his neck. When he looked down, she was standing over by the fireplace.

"Good night," she said positively, with a quick gesture of dismissal as she saw the look in his eyes.

Each of the million million men who made up the past of David, that moment reached a hand out of the distance and pushed him forward. But of them all there was none so helpless with modesty, - so in need of hiding from every eye, - even his own, - the sacred annals of that moment.

He was standing by the table on which burned the candles. He bent down quickly and blew them out and went over to her by the dim firelight.

XIX

All high happiness has in it some element of love; all love contains a desire for peace. One immediate effect of new happiness, new love, is to make us turn toward the past with a wish to straighten out its difficulties, heal its breaches, forgive its wrongs. We think most hopefully of distressing things which may still be remedied, most regretfully of others that have passed beyond our reach and will.

It was between ten and eleven o'clock of the next day - Sunday. David's cold had become worse. He had turned over necessary work to the negro man and stayed quietly in his room since the silent breakfast Two or three books chosen carelessly out of the trunk lay on his table before the fire: interest had gone out of them this day. With his face red and swollen, he was sitting beside this table with one hand loosely covering the forgotten books, his eyes turned to the window, but looking upon distant inward scenes.

Sunday morning between ten and eleven o'clock! the church-going hour of his Bible-student life. In imagination he could hear across these wide leagues of winter land the faint, faint peals of the church bells which were now ringing. He was back in the town again - up at the college - in his room at the dormitory; and it was in the days before the times of his trouble.

The students were getting ready for church, with freshly shaved faces, boots well blacked, best suits on, not always good ones. He could hear their talk in the rooms around his, hear fragments of hymns, the opening and shutting of doors along the hallways, and the running of feet down the stairs. By ones and twos and larger groups they passed down and out with their hymnals, Testaments, sometimes blank books for notes on the sermon. Several thrust bright, cordial faces in at the door, as they passed, to see whether he and his roommate had started.

The scene changed. He was in the church, which was crowded from pulpit to walls. He was sitting under the chandelier in the choir, the number of the first hymn had just been whispered along, and he began to sing, with hundreds of others, the music which then released the pinions of his love and faith as the air releases the wings of a bird. The hymn ceased; he could see the pastor rise from behind the pulpit, advance, and with a gesture gather that sea of heads to prayer. He could follow the sermon, most of all the exhortation; around him was such stillness in the church that his own heart-beats were audible. Then the Supper and then home to the dormitory again - with a pain of happiness filling him, the rest and the unrest of consecration.

Many other scenes he lived through in memory this morning - once lived in reality amid that brotherhood of souls. His tenderest thoughts perhaps dwelt on the young men's prayer-meetings of Sunday afternoons at the college. There they drew nearest to the Eternal Strength which was behind their weakness, and closest to each other as student after student lifted a faltering, stumbling petition for a common blessing on their work. The Immortal seemed to be in that bare room, filling their hearts with holy flame, drawing around them the isolation of a devoted band. They were one in One. Then had followed the change in him which produced the change in them: no fellowship, no friendship, with an unbeliever; and he was left without a comrade.

His heart was yearning and sick this day to be reconciled to them all. How did they think of him, speak of him, now? Who slept in his bed? Who sat a little while, after the studies of the night were over, talking to his room-mate? Who knelt down across the room at his prayers when the lights were put out? And his professors - what bulwarks of knowledge and rectitude and kindness they were! - all with him at first, all against him at last, as in duty bound.

To one man alone among those hundreds could David look back as having begun to take interest in him toward the close of his college days. During that vacation which he had spent in reading and study, he had often refreshed himself by taking his book out to the woodland park near the city, which in those days was the grounds of one of the colleges of the University. There he found the green wild country again, a forest like his pioneer ancestor's. Regularly here he observed at out-of-door work the professor of Physical Science, who also was pressing his investigations forward during the leisure of those summer months. An authority from the north, from a New England university, who had resigned his chair to come to Kentucky, attracted by the fair prospects of the new institution. A great gray-bearded, eagle-faced, square-shouldered, big-footed man: reserved, absorbed, asking to be let alone, one of the silent masters. But David, desperate with intellectual loneliness himself, and knowing this man to be a student of the new science, one day had introduced himself and made inquiry about entering certain classes in his course the following session.

The professor shook his head. He was going back to New England himself the next year; and he moved away under the big trees, resuming his work.

As troubles had thickened about David, his case became discussed in University circles; and he was stopped on the street one day by this frigid professor and greeted with a man's grasp and a look of fresh beautiful affection. His apostasy from dogmatism had made him a friend of that lone thinker whose worship of God was the worship of Him through the laws of His universe and not through the dogmas of men.

This professor - and Gabriella: they alone, though from different motives, had been drawn to him by what had repelled all others. It was his new relation to her beyond anything else that filled David this day with his deep desire for peace with his past. She had such peace in herself, such charity of feeling, such simple steadfast faith: she cast the music of these upon the chords of his own soul. To the influence of her religion she was now adding the influence of her love; it filled him, subdued, overwhelmed him. And this morning, also out of his own happiness he remembered with most poignant suffering the unhappiness of his father. His own life was unfolding into fulness of affection and knowledge and strength; his father's was closing amid the weakness and troubles that had gathered about him; and he, David, had contributed his share to these. To be reconciled to his father this day - that was his sole thought.

It was about four o'clock. The house held that quiet which reigns of a Sunday afternoon when the servants have left the kitchen for the cabin, when all work is done, and the feeling of Sunday rest takes possession of our minds. The winter sunshine on the fields seems full of rest; the brutes rest - even those that are not beasts of burden. The birds appear to know the day, and to make note of it in quieter twitter and slower flight.

David rose resolutely and started downstairs. As he entered his father's room, his mother was passing out She looked at her son with apprehension, as she closed the door. His father was sitting by a window, reading, as was his Sunday wont, the Bible. He had once written to David that his had always been a religious people; it was true. A grave, stern man - sternest, gravest on Sunday. When it was not possible to go to church, the greater to him the reason that the house itself should become churchlike in solemnity, out of respect to the day and the duty of self-examination. A man of many failings, but on this subject strong.

David sat down and waited for him to reach the end of the page or chapter. But his father read on with a slow perceptible movement of his lips.

"Father."

The gray head was turned slowly toward him in silent resentment of the interruption.

"I thought it would be better to come down and talk with you."

The eyes resought the page , the lips resumed

their movements.

"I am sorry to interrupt you."

The eye still followed the inspired words, from left to right, left to right, left to right.

"Father, things ought not to go on in this way between us. I have been at home now for two months. I have waited, hoping that you would give me the chance to talk about it all. You have declined, and meantime I have simply been at work, as I used to be. But this must not be put off longer for several reasons. There are other things in my life now that I have to think of and care for." The tone in which David spoke these last words was unusual and significant.

The eyes stopped at a point on the page. The lips were pressed tightly together.

David rose and walked quietly out of the room. After he had closed the door behind him and put his foot on the stairs, he stopped and with fresh determination reopened the door. His father had shut the Bible, laid it on the floor at the side of his chair, and was standing in the middle of the room with his eyes on the door through which David had passed. He pointed to his son to be seated, and resumed his chair. He drew his penknife from his pocket and slowly trimmed the ravellings from his shirt-cuffs, blowing them off his wrists. David saw that his hands were trembling violently. The tragedy in the poor action cut him to the heart and he threw himself remorsefully into the midst of things.

"Father, I know I have disappointed you! Know it as

well as you do; but I could not have done differently."

"YOU not believe in Christianity! YOU not believe the Bible!"

The suppressed enraged voice summed up again the old contemptuous opinion.

The young man felt that there was another than himself whom it wounded.

"Sir, you must not speak to me with that feeling! Try to see that I am as sincere as you are. As to the goodness of my mind, I did not derive it from myself and am not to blame. I have only made an earnest and an honest use of what mind was given me. But I have not relied upon it alone. There are great men, some of the greatest minds of the world, who have been my teachers and determined my belief."

"All your life you had the word of God as your teacher and you believed it. Now these men tell you not to believe it and you believe them. And then you complain that I do not think more highly of you."

"Father," cried David, "there is one man whose name is very dear to us both. The blood of that man is in me as it is in you. Sir, it is your grandfather. Do you remember what the church of his day did with him? Do you forget that, standing across the fields yonder, is the church he himself built to freedom of opinion in religious matters? I grew up, not under the shadow of that church, for it casts none, but in the light of it. I have seen many churches worship there. I have had before me, from the time I could remember, my great-grandfather's words: they seemed to me the voice of

God by whom all men were created, and the spirit of Christ by whom, as you believe, men are to be saved."

The younger man stopped and waited in vain for the older one to reply. But his father also waited, and David went on: -

"I do not expect you to stand against the church in what it has done with me: that HAD to be done. If you had been an elder of that church, I know you, too, would have voted to expel me. What I do ask of you is that you think me as sincere in my belief as I think you in yours. I do ask for your toleration, your charity. Everything else between us will be easy, if you can see that I have done only what I could. The faith of the world grows, changes. Sons cannot always agree with their fathers; otherwise the world would stand still. You do not believe many things your own grandfather believed - the man of whose memory you are so proud. The faith you hold did not even exist among men in his day. I can no longer agree with you: I do not think the less of you because I believe differently; do not think the less of me!"

The young man could not enter into any argument with the old one. He would not have disturbed if he could his father's faith: it was too late in life for that. Neither could he defend his own views without attacking his father's: that also would have been cruelty in itself and would have been accepted as insulting. Still David could not leave his case without witnesses.

"There are things in the old Bible that no scholar now believes."

"The Almighty declares they are true; you say they are

not: I prefer to believe the Almighty. Perhaps He knows better than you and the scholars."

David fell into sorrowful silence. "There are some other matters about which I should like to speak with you, father," he said, changing the subject. "I recall one thing you said to me the day I came home. You asked me why I had come back here: do you still feel that way?"

"I do. This is a Christian house. This is a Christian community. You are out of place under this roof and in this neighborhood. Life was hard enough for your mother and me before. But we did for you what we could; you were pleased to make us this return. It will be better for you to go."

Every word seemed to have been hammered out of iron, once melted in the forge, but now cold and unchangeably shaped to its heavy purpose. The young man writhed under the hopelessness of the situation: -

"Sir, is it all on one side? Have I done nothing for you in all these years? Until I was nearly a man's age, did I not work? For my years of labor did I receive more than a bare living? Did you ever know a slave as faithful? Were you ever a harsh master to this slave? Do you owe me nothing for all those years? - I do not mean money, - I mean kindness, justice!"

"How many years before you began to work for us did your mother and I work for you? Did you owe us nothing for all that?"

"I did! I do! I always shall! But do you count it against me that Nature brought me forth helpless and kept me helpless for so many years afterwards? If my being born was a fault, whose was it? Is the dependence of an infant on its parent a debt? Father! father! Be just! be just! that you may be more kind to me."

"Kind to YOU! Just to YOU!" Hitherto his father had spoken with a quietude which was terrible, on account of the passion raging beneath. But now he sprang to his feet, strode across, and, pulling a ragged shirt-cuff down from under his coat-sleeve, shook it in his son's eyes - poverty. He went to one of the rotting doors and jerking it open without turning the knob, rattled it on its loose hinges - poverty. He turned to the window, and with one gesture depicted ruined outhouses and ruined barn, now hidden under the snow, and beautiful in the Sunday evening light - poverty. He turned and faced his son, majestic in mingled grief and care.

"Kind! just! you who have trifled with your advantages, you who are sending your mother out of her home - "

David sprang toward him in an agony of trouble and remorse.

"It is not true, it is not necessary! Father, you have been too much influenced by my mother's fears. This is Bailey's doing. It is about this I have wanted to talk to you. I shall see Bailey to-morrow."

"I forbid you to see him or to interfere."

"I must see him, whether you wish it or not," and David, to save other hard words that were coming, turned quickly and left the room.

He did not go down to supper. Toward bedtime, as he sat before his fire, he heard a slow, unfamiliar step mounting the stair. Not often in a year did he have the chance to recognize that step. His mother entered, holding a small iron stewpan, from under the cover of which steamed a sweet, spicy odor.

"This will do your cold good," she said, tasting the stew out of a spoon which she brought in her other hand, and setting it down on the hot hearth. Then she stood looking a little fearfully at her son, who had not moved. Ah, that is woman's way! She incites men to a difficulty, and then appears innocently on the battle-field with bandages for the belligerents. How many of the quarrels of this world has she caused - and how few ever witnessed!

David was sick in heart and body and kept his chair and made no reply. His mother suddenly turned, feeling a cold draft on her back, and observed the broken window-pane and the flapping sheet of paper.

"There's putty and glass in the store-room: why don't you put that pane of glass in?"

"I will sometime," said David, absently. She went over to his bed and beat up the bolster and made everything ready for him.

"You ought to have clean sheets and pillow-cases," she remarked confidently; "the negroes are worthless. Good night," she said, with her hand on the door, looking back at him timidly.

He sprang up and went over to her. "Oh, mother! mother! mother!" he cried, and then he checked the useless words that came rushing in a flood.

"Good night! and thank you for coming. Good night! Be careful, I'll bring the candle, the stairway is dark. Good night!"

"Oh, Gabriella! Gabriella!" he murmured as he went back to his table. He buried his head on his arms a moment, then, starting up, threw off his clothes, drank the mixture, and got into bed.

XX

At dead of night out in a lonely country, what sound freezes the blood like the quick cry of an animal seized and being killed? The fright, the pain, the despair: whosoever has heard these notes has listened to the wild death-music of Nature, ages old.

On the still frozen air near two or three o'clock of next morning, such a cry rang out from inside the barn. There were the short rushes to and fro, round and round; then violent leapings against the door, the troughs, and sides of the stable; then mad plunging, struggling, panting; then a long, terrified, weakened wail, which told everything beyond the clearness of words.

Up in his room, perfectly dark, for the coals in the grate were now sparkless, David was lying on his back, sleeping heavily and bathed in perspiration. Overheated, he had pushed the bed covers off from his throat; he had hollowed the pillow away from his face. So deep was the stillness of the house and of the night air outside, that almost the first sounds had reached his ear and sunk down into his brain: he stirred slightly. As the tumult grew louder, he tossed his head from side to side uneasily, and muttered a question in his broken dreams. And now the barn was in an uproar; and the dog, chained at his kennel behind the house, was howling, roaring to get loose. Would he never waken? Would the tragedy which he himself had unwittingly planned and staged be played to its end without his hearing a word? (So often it is that way in life.) At last, as one who has long tugged at his own sleep, striving to rend it as a smothering blanket and burst through into free air, he sat up in bed, confused, listening.

"Dogs!" he exclaimed, grinding his teeth.

He was out of bed in an instant, groping for his clothes. It seemed he would never find them. As he dressed, he muttered remorsefully to himself: - "I simply put them into a trap."

When he had drawn on socks, boots, and trousers, he slipped into his overcoat, felt for his hat, and hurried down. He released the dog, which instantly was off in a noiseless run, and followed, buttoning the coat about him as he went: the air was like ice against his bare, hot throat. Another moment and he could hear the dogs fighting. When he reached the door of the shed and threw it open, the flock of sheep bounded out past him in a wild rush for the open. He stepped inside, searching around with his foot as he groped. Presently it struck against something large and soft close to the wall in a corner. He reached down and taking it by the legs, pulled the sheep out into the moonlight, several yards across the snow: a red track followed, as though made with a broad dripping brush.

David stood looking down at it and kicked it two or three times.

"Did it make any difference to you whether your life were taken by dog or man? The dog killing you from instinct and famine; a man killing you as a luxury and with a fine calculation? And who is to blame now for your death, if blame there be? I who went to college instead of building a stable? Or the storm which deprived these prowlers of nearer food and started them on a far hunt, desperate with hunger? Or man who took you from wild Nature and made you more defenceless under his keeping? Or Nature herself who edged the tooth and the mind of the dog-wolf in the beginning that he might lengthen his life by shortening yours? Where and with what purpose began on this planet the taking of life that there might be life? Poor questions that never troubled you, poor sheep! But that follow, as his shadow, pondering Man, who no more knows the reason of it all than you did."

The fighting of the dogs had for the first few moments sounded farther and farther away, retreating through the barn and thence into the lot; and by and by the shepherd ran around and stood before David, awaiting orders. David seized the sheep by the feet and dragged it into the saddle-house; sent the dog to watch the rest of the flock; and ran back to the house, drawing his overcoat more tightly about him. As quickly as possible he got into bed and covered up warmly. Something caused him to recollect just then the case of one of the Bible students.

"Now I am in for it," he said.

And this made him think of his great masters and of Gabriella; and he lay there very anxious in the night.

XXI

Twilight had three times descended on the drear land. Three times Gabriella, standing at her windows and looking out upon the snow and ice, had seen everything disappear. How softly white were the snow-covered trees; how soft the black that thickened about them till they were effaced. Gabriella thought of them as still perfectly white out there in the darkness. Three evenings with her face against the pane she had watched for a familiar figure to stalk towering up the yard path, and no familiar figure had come. Three evenings she had returned to her firelight, and sat before it with an ear on guard for the sound of a familiar step on the porch below; but no step had been heard.

On the first night she had all but hoped that he would not seek her; the avowal of their love for each other had well-nigh left it an unendurable joy. But the second night she had begun to expect him confidently; and when the hour had passed and he had not come, Gabriella sat long before her fire with a new wound - she who had felt so many. By the third day she had reviewed all that she had ever heard of him or known of him: gathered it all afresh as a beautiful thing for receiving him with when he should come to her that night. Going early to her room she had taken her chair to the window and with her face close to the pane had watched again - watched that white yard; and again nothing moved in that white yard but the darkness.

She sprang up and began to walk to and fro.

"If he does not come to-night, something has happened. I know, I know, I know! Something is wrong. My heart is not mistaken. Oh, if anything were to happen to HIM! I must not think of it! I have borne many things; but THAT! I must not think of it!"

She sank into her chair with her ear strained toward the porch below. For a long time there was no sound. Then she heard the noise of heavy boots - a tapping of the toes against the pillars, to knock off the snow, and then the slow creaking of soles across the frozen boards. She started up. "It is some one else," she cried, wringing her hands. "Something has happened to him."

She stopped still in the middle of the room, her arms dropped at her sides, her eyes stretched wide.

The house girl's steps were heard running upstairs. Gabriella jerked the door open in her face.

"What is the matter?" she cried.

A negro man had come with a message for her. The girl looked frightened.

Gabriella ran past her down into the hall. "What is the matter?" she asked.

His Marse David had sent for her and wanted her to come at once. He had brought a horse for her.

"Is he ill - seriously ill?" He had had a bad cold and was worse.

"The doctor - has he sent for the doctor?"

The negro said that he was to take her back first and then go for the doctor.

"Go at once."

It was very dark, he urged, and slippery.

"Go on for the doctor! Where have you left the horse?"

The horse was at the stiles. The negro insisted that it would be better for him to go back with her.

"Don't lose time," she said, "and don't keep me waiting. Go! As quickly as you can!"

The negro cautioned her to dismount at the frozen creek.

When Gabriella, perhaps an hour later, knocked at the side door of David's home, - his father's and mother's room, - there was no summons to enter. She turned the knob and walked in. The room was empty; the fire had burned low; a cat lay on the hearthstones. It raised its head halfway and looked at her through the narrow slits of its yellow eyes and curled the tip of its tail - the cat which is never inconvenienced, which shares all comforts and no troubles. She sat down in a chair, overcome with excitement and hesitating what to do. In a moment she noticed that the door opening on the foot of the staircase stood ajar. It led to his room. Not a sound reached her from above. She summoned all her self-control, mounted the stairway, and entered.

The two negro women were standing inside with their backs to the door. On one side of the bed sat David's mother, on the other his father. Both were looking at David. He lay in the middle of the bed, his eyes fixed restlessly on the door. As soon as he saw her, he lifted himself with an effort and stretched out his arms and shook them at her with hoarse little cries. "Oh! oh! oh! oh!"

The next moment he locked his arms about her.

"Oh, it has been so long!" he said, drawing her close, "so long!"

"Ah, why did you not send for me? I have waited and waited."

He released her and fell back upon the pillows; then with a slight gesture he said to his father and mother: -

"Will you leave us alone?"

When they had gone out, he took one of her hands and pressed it against his cheek and lay looking at her piteously.

Gabriella saw the change in him: his anxious expression, his cheeks flushed with a red spot, his restlessness, his hand burning. She could feel the big veins throbbing too fast, too crowded. But a woman smiles while her heart breaks.

He propped himself a little higher on the pillows and turned on his side, clutching at his lung.

"Don't be frightened," he said, searching her face, "I've got something to tell you. Promise."

"I promise."

"I am going to have pneumonia, or I have it now. You are not frightened?"

Her eyes answered for her.

"I had a cold. I had taken something to throw me into a sweat - that was the night after I saw you."

At the thought of their last interview, he took her hand again and pressed it to his lips, looking tenderly at it.

"The dogs were killing the sheep, and I got up and went out while I was in a perspiration. I know it's pneumonia. I have had a long, hard chill. My head feels like it would burst, and there are other symptoms. This lung! It's pneumonia. One of the Bible college students had it. I helped to nurse him. Oh, he got well," he said, shaking his head at her with a smile, "and so will I!"

"I know it," she murmured, "I'm sure of it."

"What I want to ask is, Will you stay with me?"

"Ah, nothing could take me from you."

"I don't want you to leave me. I want to feel that you are right here by me through it all. I have to tell you something else: I may be delirious and not know what is going on. I have sent for the doctor. But there is a better one in Lexington. You try to get him to come. I know that he goes wherever he is called and stays till the danger is past or - or - till it is settled. Don't spare anything that can be done for me. I am in danger, and I must live. I must not lose all the greatness of life and lose you."

"Ah," she implored, seeing how ill he was. "Everything that can be done shall be done. Now oughtn't you to be quiet and let me make you comfortable till the doctor comes?"

"I must say something else while I can, and am sure. I might not get over this - "

"Ah - "

"Let me say this: I MIGHT not! If I should not, have no fear about the future; I have none; it will all be well with ME in Eternity."

He lay quiet a moment, his face turned off. She had buried hers on the bed. The flood of tears would come. He turned over, and seeing it laid his hand on it very lightly.

"If it be so, Gabriella, I hope all the rest of your life you will be happy. I hope no more trouble will ever come to you."

Suddenly he sat up, lifted her head, and threw his arms around her again. "Oh, Gabriella!" he cried, "you have been all there is to me."

"Some day," he continued a moment later, "if it turns out that way, come over here to see my father and mother. And tell them I left word that perhaps they had never quite understood me and so had never been able to do me justice. Now, will you call my mother?"

"Mother," he said, taking her by the hand and placing it in Gabriella's, "this is my wife, as I hope she will be, and your daughter; and I have asked her to stay and help you to nurse me through this cold."

Three twilights more and there was a scene in the little upper room of the farmhouse: David drawn up on the bed; at one side of it, the poor distracted mother, rocking herself and loudly weeping; for though mothers may not greatly have loved their grown sons, when the big men lie stricken and the mothers once more take their hands to wash them, bathe their faces with a cloth, put a spoon to their lips, memory brings back the days when those huge erring bodies lay across their breasts. They weep for the infant, now an infant again and perhaps falling into a long sleep.

On the other side of the bed sat David's father, bending over toward, trying now, as he had so often tried, to reach his son; thinking at swift turns of the different will he would have to make and of who would write it; of his own harshness; and also not free from the awful dread that this was the summons to his son to enter Eternity with his soul unprepared. At the foot of the bed were the two doctors, watchful, whispering to each other, one of whom led the mother out of the room; over by the door the two negro women and the negro man. Gabriella was not there.

Gabriella had gone once more to where she had been many times: gone to pour out in secret the prayer of her church, and of her own soul for the sick - with faith that her prayer would be answered.

A dark hour: a dog howling on the porch below; at the stable the cries of hungry, neglected animals; the winter hush settling over the great evening land.

XXII

When one sets out to walk daily across a wood or field in a fresh direction, starting always at the same point and arriving always at the same, without intention one makes a path; it may be long first, but in time the path will come. It commences at the home gate or bars and reaches forward by degrees; it commences at the opposite goal and lengthens backward thence: some day the ends meet and we discover with surprise how slightly we have deviated in all those crossings and recrossings. The mind has unconsciously marked a path long before the feet have traced it.

When Gabriella had begun teaching, she passed daily out of the yard into an apple orchard and thence across a large woodland pasture, in the remote corner of which the schoolhouse was situated. Through this woods the children had made their path: the straight instinctive path of childhood. But Gabriella, leaving this at the woods-gate, had begun to make one for herself. She followed her will from day to day; now led in this direction by some better vista; now drawn aside toward a group of finer trees; or seeing, farther on, some little nooklike place. In time, she had out of short disjointed threads sown a continuous path; it was made up of her loves, and she loved it. Of mornings a brisk walk along this braced her mind for the day; in the evening it quieted jangled nerves and revived a

James Lane Allen

worn-out spirit: shedding her toil at the schoolhouse door as a heavy suffocating garment, she stepped gratefully out into its largeness, its woodland odors, and twilight peace.

On the night of the sleet tons of timber altogether had descended across this by-way. When the snow fell the next night, it brought down more. But the snow melted, leaving the ice; the ice melted, leaving the dripping boughs and bark. In time these were warmed and dried by sun and wind. New edges of greenness appeared running along the path. The tree-tops above were tossing and roaring in the wild gales of March, Under loose autumn leaves the earliest violets were dim with blue. But Gabriella had never once been there to realize how her path had been ruined, or to note the birth of spring.

It was perhaps a month afterward that one morning at the usual school hour her tall lithe figure, clad in gray hood and cloak, appeared at last walking along this path, stepping over or passing around the fallen boughs. She was pale and thin, but the sweet warm womanliness of her, if possible, lovelier. There was a look of religious gratitude in the eyes, but about her mouth new happiness.

Her duties were done earlier than usual that afternoon, for not much could be accomplished on this first day of reassembling the children. They were gone; and she stood on the steps of the school-house, facing toward a gray field on a distant hillside, which caught the faint sunshine. It drew her irresistibly in heart and foot, and she set out toward it.

The day was one of those on which the seasons meet.

Strips of snow ermined the field; but on the stumps, wandering and warbling before Gabriella as she advanced, were bluebirds, those wings of the sky, those breasts of earth. She reached the spot she was seeking, and paused. There it was - the whole pitiful scene! His hemp brake; the charred rind of a stump where he had kindled a fire to warm his hands; the remnant of the shock fallen over and left unfinished that last afternoon; trailing across his brake a handful of hemp partly broken out.

She surveyed it all with wistful tenderness. Then she looked away to the house. She could see the window of his room at which she had sat how many days, gazing out toward this field! On his bed in that room he was now stretched weak and white, but struggling back into health.

She came closer and gazed down at his frozen boot prints. How near his feet had drawn to that long colder path which would have carried him away from her. How nearly had his young life been left, like the hand of hemp he last had handled - half broken out, not yet ready for strong use and good service. At that moment one scene rose before her memory: a day at Bethlehem nigh Jerusalem; a young Hebrew girl issuing from her stricken house and hastening to meet Him who was the Resurrection and the Life; then in her despair uttering her one cry: - "Lord, if Thou hadst been here, my brother had not died."

The mist of tears blinded Gabriella, whose love and faith were as Martha's. She knelt down and laid her cheek against the coarse hemp where it had been wrapped about his wrist.

"Lord," she said, "hadst Thou not been here, hadst Thou not heard my prayer for him, he would have died!"

XXIII

Spring, who breaks all promises in the beginning to keep them in the end, had ceased from chilling caprice and withdrawals: the whole land was now the frank revelation of her loveliness. Autumn - the hours of falling and of departing; spring - season of rise and of return. The rise of sap from root to summit; the rise of plant from soil to sun; the rise of bud from bark to bloom; the rise of song from heart to hearing: vital days. And days when things that went away come back, when woods, fields, thickets, and streams are full of returns.

Gabriella was not disappointed. Those provident old tree-mothers on the orchard slope, whose red-cheeked children are autumn apples, had not let themselves be fatally surprised by the great February frost: their bark-cradled bud-infants had only been wrapped away the more warmly till danger was over. For many days now the hillside had been a grove of pink and white domes under each of which hung faint fragrance: the great silent marriage-bells of the trees.

After the early family supper, Gabriella, if there had been no shower, would take her shawl to sit on and some bit of work for companionship. She would go out to the edge of this orchard away from the tumult of the house. The hill sloped down into a wide green valley winding away toward the forest below. Through this valley a stream of white spring water, drunk by the stock, ran within banks of mint and over a bed of rocks and moss. On the hillside opposite was a field of young hemp stretching westward - soon to be a low sea of rippling green. Beyond this field was the sunset; over it flashed the evening star; and for the past few days beside the star had hung the inconstant, the constant, crescent of ages.

She liked to spread her shawl on the edge of the orchard overlooking the valley - a deep carpet of grass sprinkled with wind-blown petals; to watch the sky kindle and burn out; see the recluse Evening come forth before the Night and walk softly down the valley toward the woods; feel as an elixir about her the air, sweet from the trees, sweet with earth odors, sweet with all the lingering history of the day. Nearer, ever nearer would swing the stars into her view. The moon, late a bow of thinnest, mistiest silver, now of broadening, brightening gold, would begin to drive the darkness downward from the white domes of the trees till it lay as a faint shadow beneath them. These were hours fraught with peace and rest to her tired mind and tired body.

One day she was sitting thus, absently knitting herself some bleaching gloves, (Gabriella's hands were as if stained by all the mixed petals of the boughs.) The sun was going down beyond the low hills, In the orchard behind her she could hear the flutter of wings and the last calls of quieting birds.

She had dropped the threads of her handiwork into her lap, and with folded hands was knitting memories.

At twilights such as this in years gone by, she, a little girl, had been used to drive out into the country with her grandmother - often choosing the routes herself and ordering the carriage to be stopped on the road as her fancy pleased. For in those aristocratic days, Southern children, like those of royal families, were encouraged early in life to learn how to give orders and to exact obedience and to rule: when they grew up they would have many under them: and not to reign was to be ruined. So that the infantile autocrat Gabriella was being instructed in this way and in that way by the powerful, strong-minded, efficient grandmother as a tender old lioness might train a cub for the mastering of its dangerous world. She recalled these twilight drives when the fields along the turnpikes were turning green with the young grain; the homeward return through the lamp-lit town to the big iron entrance-gate, the parklike lawn; the brilliant supper in the great house, the noiseless movements, the perfect manners of the many servants; later in the evening the music, the dancing, the wild joy - fairyland once more. But how far, far away now! And how the forces of life had tossed things since then like straws on the eddies of a tempest: her grandmother killed, thousands of miles away, with sorrow; her uncles with their oldest sons, mere boys, fighting and falling together; tears, poverty, ruin everywhere: and she, after years of struggle, cast completely out of the only world she had ever known into another that she had never imagined.

Gabriella felt this evening what often came to her at times: a deep yearning for her own people of the past, for their voices, their ways of looking at life; for the gentleness and courtesy, and the thousand unconscious moods and acts that rendered them distinguished and delightful. She would have liked to slip back into the

James Lane Allen

old elegance, to have been surrounded by the old rich and beautiful things. The child-princess who was once her sole self was destined to live within Gabriella always.

But she knew that the society in which she had moved was lost to her finally. Not alone through the vicissitudes of the war; for after the war, despite the overthrow, the almost complete disappearance, of many families, it had come together, it had reconstituted itself, it flourished still. It was lost to her because she had become penniless and because she had gone to work. When it transpired that she had declined all aid, thrown off all disguises, and taken her future into her own hands, to work and to receive wages for her work, in the social world where she was known and where the generations of her family had been leaders, there were kind offers of aid, secret condolences, whispered regrets, visible distress: her resolve was a new thing for a girl in those years. She could, indeed, in a way, have kept her place; but she could not have endured the sympathy, the change, with which she would have been welcomed - and discarded. She made trial of this a few times and was convinced: up to the day of the cruel discovery of that, Gabriella had never dreamed what her social world could be to one who had dropped out of it.

Her church and the new life - these two had been left her. She no longer had a pew, but she had her faith and this was enough; for it always gave her, wherever she was, some secret place in which to kneel and from which to rise strengthened and comforted. As for the fearful fields of work into which she had come, a strange and solitary learner, these had turned into the abiding, the living landscapes of life now. Here she had found independence - sweet, wholesome crust; found another self within herself; and here found her mission for the future - David. So that looking upon the disordered and planless years, during which it had often seemed that she was struggling unwatched, Gabriella now believed that through them she had most been guided, When many hands had let hers go, One had taken it; when old pathways were closed, a new one was opened; and she had been led along it - home.

David's illness had deepened beyond any other experience her faith in an overruling Providence. His return to health was to her a return from death: it was an answer to her prayers: it was a resurrection. Henceforth his life was a gift for the second time to himself, to her, to the world for which he must work with all his powers and work aright. And her pledge, her compact with the Divine, was to help him, to guide him back into the faith from which he had wandered. Outside of prayer, days and nights at his bedside had made him hers: vigils, nursing, suffering, helplessness, dependence - all these had been as purest oil to that alabaster lamp of love which burned within her chaste soul.

The sun had gone down. The hush of twilight was descending from the clear sky, in the depths of which the brightest stars began to appear as points of silvery flame. The air had the balm of early summer, the ground was dry and warm.

Gabriella began to watch. The last time she had gone to see him, as he walked part of the way back with her, he had said: -

"I am well now; the next time *I* am coming to

see YOU."

Soon, along the edge of the orchard from the direction of the house, she saw him walking slowly toward her, thin, gaunt; he was leaning on a rough, stout hickory, as long as himself, in the manner of an old man.

She rose quickly and hastened to him. "Did you walk?"

"I rode. But I am walking now - barely. This young tree is escorting me."

They went back to her shawl, which she opened and spread, making a place for him. She moved it back a little, for safety, so that it was under the boughs of one of the trees.

How quiet the land was, how beautiful the evening light, how sweet the air!

Now and then a petal from some finished blossom sifted down on Gabriella.

They were at such peace: their talk was interrupted by the long silences which are peace.

"Gabriella, you saved my life."

"It is not I who have power over life and death."

"It was your nursing."

"It was my prayers," murmured Gabriella.

"And you gave me the will to get well: that also was a great help: without you I should not have had that same will to live."

"It was a higher Will than yours or mine."

"And the doctor from town who stayed with me."

"And a Greater Physician who stayed also."

He made no reply for a while, but then asked, turning his face toward her uneasily: -

"Our different ways of looking at things - will they never make any difference with you?"

"Some day there will be no difference."

"You will agree with me?" he exclaimed joyfully.

"You will agree with me."

"Do not expect that! Do not expect that I shall ever again believe in the old things."

"I expect you to believe in God, in the New Testament, in the Resurrection, in the answer to prayer."

"If I do not?"

"Then you will in the Life to come."

"But will this separate us?"

"You will need me all the more."

The light was fading: they could no longer see the green of the valley. A late bird fluttered into the boughs overhead and more petals came down.

"It is a nest," said David, softly, "a good thing to go home to, a night like this."

"And now," he continued, "there are matters about which I must consult you. You will be glad to know that things are pleasanter at home. Since my illness my father and mother have changed toward me. Sickness, nearness to death, is a great reconciler. Your being in the house had much to do with this - especially your influence over my mother. My father was talked to by the doctor from town. During the days and nights he stayed with me, he got into my trunk of books, for he is a great reader; and - as he told me before leaving - a believer in the New Science, an evolutionist. He knew of my expulsion, of course, and of the reasons. I think he explained a great deal to my father, who said to me one day simply that the doctor had talked to him."

"He talked to me, also," said Gabriella. "And did not persuade you?"

"He said I almost persuaded him!"

"And then, too, my father and I have arranged the money trouble. It is not the best, but the best possible. When I came home from college, I brought with me almost half the money I had accumulated. I turned this over to my father, of course. It will go toward making necessary repairs. But it was not enough, and the woods has had to go. The farm shall not be sold, but the woods is rented for a term of years as hemp land, the trees must be deadened and cut down. I am sorry; it is the last of the forest of my great-grandfather. But with the proceeds, the place can be put into fairly good condition, and this is the greatest relief to my father and mother - and to me."

"It is a good arrangement."

After a pause, he continued in a changed tone: -

"And now while everything is pleasant at home, it is the time for me to go away. My father was right: this is no place for me. I must be where people think as I do - must live where I shall not be alone. There will soon be plenty of companions everywhere. The whole world will believe in Evolution before I am an old man."

"I think you are right," she said quietly. "It is best for you to go and to go at once."

When he spoke again, plainly he was inspired with fresh confidence by her support of his plans.

"And now, Gabriella, I must tell you what I have determined to do in life: I want your approval of that, and then I am perfectly happy."

"Ah," she said quickly, "that is what I have been wanting to know. It is very important. Your whole future depends on a wise choice."

"I am going to some college - to some northern university, as soon as possible. I shall have to work my way through, sometimes by teaching, in whatever way I can. I want to study physical science. I want to teach some branch of it. It draws me, draws all that is in me. That is to be my life-work. And now?"

He waited for her answer: it did not come at once.

"You have chosen wisely. I am so glad!"

"Oh, Gabriella!" he cried, "if you had failed me in that, I do not know what I should have done! Science! Science! There is the fresh path for the faith of the race! For the race henceforth must get its idea of God, and build its religion to Him, from its knowledge of the laws of His universe. A million years from now! Where will our dark theological dogmas be in that radiant time? The Creator of all life, in all life He must be studied! And in the study of science there is least wrangling, least tyranny, least bigotry, no persecution. It teaches charity, it teaches a well-ordered life, it teaches the world to be more kind. It is the great new path of knowledge into the future. All things must follow whither it leads. Our religion will more and more be what our science is, and some day they will be the same."

She had no controversy to raise with him about this. She was too intently thinking of troublous problems nearer heart and home.

And these rose before him also: he fell into silence.

"But, oh, Gabriella! how long, how long the years will be that separate me from you!"

"No!" she exclaimed, her whole nature starting up, terrified. "What do you mean? No!"

"I mean while I am going through college; while I am preparing a place for you."

"Preparing a place FOR ME! You have prepared a place for me and I have taken it. My place is with you."

"Gabriella, do you know I have not a dollar in the world?"

"*I* have!"

"But - "

"Ah, don't! don't! That would be the first time you had ever wounded me!"

"How can I - "

"How can you go away and leave me here - here - anywhere - alone - struggling in the world alone? And you somewhere else alone? Lose those years of being together? Can you even bear the thought of it? Ah, I did not think this!"

"It was only because - "

"But it shall never be! I will not be separated from you!"

David remembered a middle-aged man at the University, working his way through college with his wife beside him. His heart melted in joy and tenderness - before the possibility of life with her so near. He could not speak.

"I will never be separated from you!"

And then, feeling her victory won, she added joyously: "And what I have shall never be separated from me! We three - I, thou, it - go together. My two years' salary - do you think I love it so little as to leave it behind when I go away with you?"

"Oh, Gabriella!" -

The domes of the trees were white with blossoms now and with moonlight. How warm and sweet the air! How sacred the words and the silences! Two children of vast and distant revolutions guided together into one life - a young pair facing toward a future of wider, better things for mankind.

"Gabriella, when a man has heard the great things calling to him, how they call and call, day and night, day and night!"

"When a woman hears them once, it is enough."

Even in this hour Gabriella was receiving the wound which is so often the pathos and the happiness of a woman's love. For even in these moments he could not forget Truth for her. And so, she said to herself with a hidden tear, it would be always. She would give him her all, she could never be all to him. Her life would be enfolded completely in his; but he would hold out his arms also toward a cold Spirit who would forever elude him - Wisdom.

The golden crescent dropped behind the dark green hills of the silent land. Where were they? Gone? or still under the trees?

"Ah, Gabriella, it is love that makes a man believe in a God of Love!"

"David! David!" -

The south wind, warm with the first thrill of summer, blew from across the valley, from across the mighty rushing sea of the young hemp.

O Mystery Immortal! which is in the hemp and in our souls, in its bloom and in our passions; by which our poor brief lives are led upward out of the earth for a season, then cut down, rotted and broken - for Thy long service!

Choose from Thousands of 1stWorldLibrary Classics By

Adolphus WilliamWard
Aesop
Agatha Christie
Alexander Aaronsohn
Alexander Kielland
Alexandre Dumas
Alfred Gatty
Alfred Ollivant
Alice Duer Miller
Alice Turner Curtis
Alice Dunbar
Ambrose Bierce
Amelia E. Barr
Andrew Lang
Andrew McFarland Davis
Anna Sewell
Annie Besant
Annie Hamilton Donnell
Annie Payson Call
Anton Chekhov
Arnold Bennett
Arthur Conan Doyle
Arthur Ransome
Atticus
B. M. Bower
Basil King
Bayard Taylor
Ben Macomber
Booth Tarkington
Bram Stoker
C. Collodi
C. E. Orr
C. M. Ingleby
Carolyn Wells
Catherine Parr Traill
Charles A. Eastman
Charles Dickens
Charles Dudley Warner
Charles Farrar Browne
Charles Ives
Charles Kingsley
Charles Lathrop Pack
Charles Whibley
Charles Willing Beale
Charlotte M. Braeme
Charlotte M.Yonge
Clair W. Hayes
Clarence Day Jr.
Clarence E. Mulford

Clemence Housman
Confucius
Cornelis DeWitt Wilcox
Cyril Burleigh
D. H. Lawrence
Daniel Defoe
David Garnett
Don Carlos Janes
Donald Keyhole
Dorothy Kilner
Dougan Clark
E. Nesbit
E.P.Roe
E. Phillips Oppenheim
Edgar Allan Poe
Edgar Rice Burroughs
Edith Wharton
Edward J. O'Biren
John Cournos
Edwin L. Arnold
Eleanor Atkins
Elizabeth Cleghorn
Gaskell
Elizabeth Von Arnim
Ellem Key
Emily Dickinson
Erasmus W. Jones
Ernie Howard Pie
Ethel Turner
Ethel Watts Mumford
Eugenie Foa
Eugene Wood
Evelyn Everett-Green
Everard Cotes
F. J. Cross
Federick Austin Ogg
Ferdinand Ossendowski
Francis Bacon
Francis Darwin
Frances Hodgson Burnett
Frank Gee Patchin
Frank Harris
Frank Jewett Mather
Frank L. Packard
Frederick Trevor Hill
Frederick Winslow Taylor
Friedrich Kerst
Friedrich Nietzsche
Fyodor Dostoyevsky

Gabrielle E. Jackson
Garrett P. Serviss
Gaston Leroux
George Ade
Geroge Bernard Shaw
George Ebers
George Eliot
George MacDonald
George Orwell
George Tucker
George W. Cable
George Wharton James
Gertrude Atherton
Grace E. King
Grant Allen
Guillermo A. Sherwell
Gulielma Zollinger
Gustav Flaubert
H. A. Cody
H. B. Irving
H. G. Wells
H. H. Munro
H. Irving Hancock
H. Rider Haggard
H. W. C. Davis
Hamilton Wright Mabie
Hans Christian Andersen
Harold Avery
Harold McGrath
Harriet Beecher Stowe
Harry Houidini
Helent Hunt Jackson
Helen Nicolay
Hendy David Thoreau
Henrik Ibsen
Henry Adams
Henry Ford
Henry Frost
Henry James
Henry Jones Ford
Henry Seton Merriman
Henry Wadsworth
Longfellow
Henry W Longfellow
Herbert A. Giles
Herbert N. Casson
Herman Hesse
Homer
Honore De Balzac

Horace Walpole
Horatio Alger, Jr.
Howard Pyle
Howard R. Garis
Hugh Lofting
Hugh Walpole
Humphry Ward
Ian Maclaren
Israel Abrahams
J.G.Austin
J. Henri Fabre
J. M. Barrie
J. Macdonald Oxley
J. S. Knowles
J. Storer Clouston
Jack London
Jacob Abbott
James Allen
James Lane Allen
James Andrews
James Baldwin
James DeMille
James Joyce
James Oliver Curwood
James Oppenheim
James Otis
Jane Austen
Jens Peter Jacobsen
Jerome K. Jerome
John Burroughs
John F. Kennedy
John Gay
John Glasworthy
John Habberton
John Joy Bell
John Milton
John Philip Sousa
Jonathan Swift
Joseph Carey
Joseph Conrad
Joseph Jacobs
Julian Hawthrone
Julies Vernes
Justin Huntly McCarthy
Kakuzo Okakura
Kenneth Grahame
Kate Langley Bosher
L. A. Abbot
L. T. Meade
L. Frank Baum
Laura Lee Hope

Laurence Housman
Leo Tolstoy
Leonid Andreyev
Lewis Carroll
Lilian Bell
Lloyd Osbourne
Louis Tracy
Louisa May Alcott
Lucy Fitch Perkins
Lucy Maud Montgomery
Lydia Miller Middleton
Lyndon Orr
M. H. Adams
Margaret E. Sangster
Margaret Vandercook
Maria Edgeworth
Maria Thompson Daviess
Mariano Azuela
Marion Polk Angellotti
Mark Overton
Mark Twain
Mary Austin
Mary Cole
Mary Rowlandson
Mary Wollstonecraft
Shelley
Max Beerbohm
Myra Kelly
Nathaniel Hawthrone
O. F. Walton
Oscar Wilde
Owen Johnson
P.G.Wodehouse
Paul and Mable Thorn
Paul G. Tomlinson
Paul Severing
Peter B. Kyne
Plato
R. Derby Holmes
R. L. Stevenson
Rabindranath Tagore
Rahul Alvares
Ralph Waldo Emmerson
Rene Descartes
Rex E. Beach
Richard Harding Davis
Richard Jefferies
Robert Barr
Robert Frost
Robert Gordon Anderson
Robert L. Drake

Robert Lansing
Robert Michael Ballantyne
Robert W. Chambers
Rosa Nouchette Carey
Ross Kay
Rudyard Kipling
Samuel B. Allison
Samuel Hopkins Adams
Sarah Bernhardt
Selma Lagerlof
Sherwood Anderson
Sigmund Freud
Standish O'Grady
Stanley Weyman
Stella Benson
Stephen Crane
Stewart Edward White
Stijn Streuvels
Swami Abhedananda
Swami Parmananda
T. S. Ackland
The Princess Der Ling
Thomas A. Janvier
Thomas A Kempis
Thomas Anderton
Thomas Bailey Aldrich
Thomas Bulfinch
Thomas De Quincey
Thomas H. Huxley
Thomas Hardy
Thomas More
Thornton W. Burgess
U. S. Grant
Valentine Williams
Victor Appleton
Virginia Woolf
Walter Scott
Washington Irving
Wilbur Lawton
Wilkie Collins
Willa Cather
Willard F. Baker
William Makepeace
Thackeray
William W. Walter
Winston Churchill
Yei Theodora Ozaki
Young E. Allison
Zane Grey